I0598850

Jake Stellar
Dead in the Water

Jake Stellar
Dead in the Water

By

Rodney Riesel

Published by Island Holiday Publishing
East Greenbush, NY

Copyright © 2017 Rodney Riesel

All rights reserved

ISBN: 978-0-9971149-7-3

First Edition

This is a work of fiction. Names, characters, businesses, places, events, and incidents either are the product of the author's imagination or are used fictitiously. Any resemblance to actual persons, living or dead, events or locales is purely coincidental.

Special thanks to:

Pamela Guerriere

Kevin Cook

Pamela Stagliano

Cover Photo by:

Joe Stagliano

Cover Design by:

Connie Fitsik

To learn about my other books friend me at

https://www.facebook.com/rodneyriesel

For Brenda,
Kayleigh, Ethan
& Peyton

Chapter One

It was a Saturday morning and the night before we had discussed going for a run. Luckily, when I got up it was cloudy and there was just enough mist in the air to cancel that idea. I suggested going out for breakfast and Bree agreed. She said she would be ready to leave in about fifteen minutes; it had been half an hour. I was ready in ten minutes.

I sat in my recliner watching The Weather Channel. Meteorologist/hurricane specialist Carl Parker was explaining a map that showed the projected path of Hurricane Petrov. He moved back and forth in front of the HD monitors. He pointed out the eye of the storm and imitated the spinning clouds using his arms and hands. He was much too excited. Overall, it took him about eight minutes to let me know that the hurricane may or may not make landfall. By the time the screen went dark and the commercial began, I didn't know much more about Petrov than I did before I had turned on the TV.

I wondered if there had ever been a Hurricane Jake; I didn't remember one. I bet if there was a Hurricane Bree it would probably make landfall two days late. *What the hell is she doing in there?*

Woofie, our miniature Yorkie, sat on my lap. I didn't think the dog was a good idea when Bree first brought it home, but it had grown on me. I often found myself speaking to it in baby talk, and on occasion referring to myself as "Daddy." I was amazed at how a four-pound dog could turn a two-hundred-pound man into an idiot.

It was the first week of October and Woofie was wearing a black sweater that said I LOVE MUMMY across the back. I was a little jealous that it didn't say I Love Daddy, but I guess that wouldn't make much sense.

"Ready when you are," I heard Bree call out as she walked down the hall.

Woofie jumped off my lap and ran to Bree. That dog only loves me when Bree isn't in the room.

"Been ready for half an hour," I replied. I pushed down the foot rest and climbed out of the chair. When I walked into the kitchen, Bree was side-stepping back and forth as Woofie danced on her hind-legs. "Look how long she can stand on two legs," Bree said.

"Yeah," I responded. "If I didn't know any better, I would say that dog landed here in a spacecraft from Krypton."

Bree shot me a look that let me know she had no idea what I was talking about. "What is that, something from *Star Track*?" she asked.

"That's *Trek* … and just for your information, Krypto was Superman's dog, who came to earth in a rocket built by Superman's father, Kal-El—oh, never mind." It wasn't my responsibility to make sure she knew the complete mythology of Superman.

I headed for the door that led from the kitchen to the garage. "Where's your keys?" I asked. They were supposed to be on one of the hooks next to the door, but they never were. They were probably at the bottom of her purse. She usually digs through her purse for a few minutes and then says "They're not in here." Then we search the entire house until she says, "Here they are. They were in my purse."

"I don't have any gas in my car," Bree informed me.

"Of course you don't," I replied. I grabbed my truck keys from the hook where they were supposed to be.

We had decided earlier to go to the Plantation Pancake House on North Kings Highway; it was our favorite place for breakfast. As I walked through the door and into the garage I hit the button and the over-head door lifted.

The sunlight filled the garage and Bree said, "It's getting nice out, Jake. We should have run."

"Too late now," I said, trying to show disappointment.

We climbed in my truck, backed out of the

driveway, and headed up Twenty-Fifth Avenue toward North Kings Highway.

"Should've run," Bree repeated.

I took a right on Madison Drive, drove a few blocks, and then pulled into the parking lot from the rear.

When I pulled open the door to the pancake house, Bree stepped back and said, "You go first."

I nodded my head toward the door. "Just go."

She shook her head and went in. "Why do you always do that? You know I like you to walk in first."

"What if there's a vicious dog in there?" I joked.

"My hero."

Millie stood behind the register, her hair in a bun with a number two pencil jabbed through it. She glanced up from a guest check. "Good morning, Stellars," she said cheerfully.

"Morning, Millie," Bree said.

"Booth?" Millie asked, knowing I hate sitting at a table in the middle of the room.

"You know it," I replied.

We followed her to the same booth where we had eaten the last three times we were there. "Here ya go," she said. "Y'all want coffee this morning?"

"Yes, please," Bree answered.

"I'll be right back with that, and Susan will be your waitress."

"Susan?" I inquired.

"She's new," Millie informed me. "But don't worry, I'll let her know the size of her tip depends on how loud she laughs at your corny jokes."

Bree snickered.

My cell phone vibrated against my thigh. I pulled it from my front pocket and looked at the number; it was Detective Gwen Lawrence. "Yeah?" I said. "Where. Okay. I'll be right there." I gave Bree that "I'm-really-sorry" look that I had given her so many times in the past. "I gotta—"

"I know," she said. "I'm gonna stay and eat. I'll walk home after."

"Are you sure?"

"It's only a few blocks." She paused and added wryly: "Maybe I'll run."

I stood and shoved my cell back into my pocket, leaned over and gave Bree a peck on the cheek. "I'll call you later. Love ya."

"I love you." She smiled.

I was out the door.

Chapter Two

The two-story home that sat at the corner of Thirteenth Avenue North and North Ocean Boulevard was about three and a half miles from the Plantation Pancake House, so it didn't take me much more than five minutes to get there. I was glad we had taken my truck to breakfast and not Bree's car, because then I would have had to stop for gas along the way.

I pulled into the wide blacktop driveway behind a North Myrtle Beach patrol car and shut off the engine. A Horry County Coroner's Office van was backed into the driveway next to the patrol car. An ambulance, as well as two more cruisers and an emergency vehicle from the fire department were parked in the street; all of their light bars were flashing. Two unmarked units sat around the corner on North Ocean Boulevard.

The driveway ran up to a two-stall garage that made up half of the first floor. The second story of the home was gray vinyl siding and the bottom story was red brick. A black, six-foot wrought-iron fence ran around the backyard, which allowed me an unobstructed view of the in-ground pool. Gwen had told me on the phone that the victim was a floater.

I climbed out of the truck, walked up the driveway, and along a concrete sidewalk that lead to a gate in the fence. I glanced back over my shoulder at the neighbors who had gathered in their front yards. Two officers spoke with two different groups of on-lookers. Each cop had a pen in one hand and a note pad in the other.

Detective Dill Perkins stood at the edge of the pool; he glanced over when he caught sight of me out of the corner of his eye. He turned and made his way toward the gate.

"Hey, Jake," Perkins said.

"Hey, Perkins," I replied. "What do we got?"

Perkins released the locking mechanism and I pulled open the gate. We walked together toward the body bag that was lying on the concrete apron, about three feet from the edge of the pool. Tommy Powers, with the coroner's office, was the medical examiner on the scene. He had just zipped the bag closed and was getting to his feet.

"Victim's name is Wanda Truman," Perkins reported. "Forty-eight years old. The kid who mows their lawn and cleans their pool found her when he got here for work this morning." Perkins glanced down at the note pad he was holding. "Kid's name is Terry Blasting."

"Kid?" I asked. "How old?"

Perkins looked to his notes once again. "Seventeen."

"He in school?"

"Senior at North Myrtle."

When we got to the pool we watched as the ambulance crew loaded the body bag onto a gurney. Gwen Lawrence stood next to Powers.

"Cause of death?" I asked.

"Poor swimmer," Powers replied.

"So she drowned?"

"Looks like it, but I'll know more when I get her on the table."

I unzipped the bag about eight inches and pulled open the flap. Wanda Truman was blue-gray and pruned. Her blond bangs did little to hide the lump and the three-inch cut on her forehead, over her left eye. "Time of death?" I asked, re-zipping.

"I would say between eight and ten last night."

"So she was out here all night?" I asked. "No one came looking for her? She married?"

Gwen nodded. "Yeah, but her husband—John Truman—is out of town on business. According to one of the neighbors, and the kid who discovered the body, he's due back later this morning."

"What's he do?"

"Commercial real estate," said Perkins. "We weren't able to reach him by phone. He's on a flight arriving at eleven. I sent a unit to meet him at his gate."

"Any children?" I asked.

"None," said Gwen.

"Pool boy have an alibi?" I asked.

"Says he and a couple other kids were at a friend's house studying last night," Gwen replied.

"Studying on Friday night?" I asked suspiciously. "His education must be very important to him. Where's he at?"

"He's inside," Perkins said. "I have a uniform in there with him."

"You and Gwen get the names of his study group and check on that alibi."

"You got it," Perkins responded. He nodded his head toward the back door of the house and he and Gwen headed that way.

When they were almost to the house I called out, "Did you call Lint?"

"He's up at his camp," Perkins hollered back. "I tried his cell phone a few times but I can't get through."

"Keep trying," I said.

"You got it."

I walked back through the gate and out into the street. I stood there and waited for one of the two officers who were questioning neighbors to notice me. One finally did.

"Thank you for you cooperation," Officer Pat Murray said to the small group he was speaking with. He turned and walked toward me. "Hey, Jake."

"Hey, Pat," I replied. "They have anything for us?"

Pat flipped open his note pad. "Not much. The victim and her husband have lived here for about a year. Wife doesn't work. Husband is in real estate—travels a lot. The kid that found her—as far as the neighbors know—has worked for them about four months now, maybe a little more."

"Any evidence of domestic trouble?"

"I asked. They said not that they know of. The lady that lives right across the street over there said the victim was real nice but the husband is quiet and kind of keeps to himself. *That* woman's husband said the victim's husband seems like"—Pat referred to his notes again—"a dick."

"A dick?"

"Yeah, he said he doesn't talk much or even wave when he gets out of his car."

"What a dick."

"Another guy, who lives next door to the couple I interviewed, said that the guy was kind of a hot-head. Said he saw him in the front yard beating a lawnmower with a two-by-four once, because it wouldn't start."

"Sounds like a hot-head."

"Probably why they hired someone to mow their lawn."

I chuckled. "Yeah, probably."

Officer Ronnie Pierce, Pat's partner, joined us when he was finished questioning *his* group of neighbors.

"Find out anything?" I asked.

"About what?" Pierce replied.

Murray shook his head. "Jesus Christ, Ronnie, did they give you any useful information we can use to solve the mystery of the dead lady in the pool?"

When it clicked, Ronnie grinned and said, "Not really. Although one guy said he saw the victim's husband beat the shit out of his lawnmower once. I think he might have an anger problem."

"Ya think?" Pat asked.

I turned and made my way back through the gate, and around to a rear sliding glass door; it was open.

Detectives Lawrence and Perkins stood in the middle of the living room. A young boy sat on the sofa in front of them; he was pale and looked nervous. Who wouldn't be under these circumstances? The kid was wearing a pair of camouflage cargo shorts and a navy-blue T-shirt with the picture of a police call box on the front. I knew what the shirt meant, but I would wait until Perkins and Gwen left before I revealed that information. I only let on that I'm a nerd in the company of other nerds.

Gwen closed the pad. "Thanks, Terry," she said.

Perkins turned to me. "We'll hunt these other two kids down and see if we can get some answers."

"Sounds good. Anybody call this kids parents?" I asked.

"Yes," Gwen answered. "Haven't been able to get a hold of them. Kid said they were home when he left this morning but doesn't know where they would be now. I left a message on their machine and I'll keep trying."

"Okay," I said. "Keep in touch."

"You got it," Perkins replied. They walked out through the slider.

I went over to the rear picture window that over-looked the backyard. I leaned forward and craned my neck to see the pool. "The yard looks real nice," I said.

"What?" Terry asked.

"The yard," I repeated. "It looks really nice. They said you took care of the property."

"Oh … yeah. Thanks."

"This the only yard you do?"

"I do the front yard too."

"I mean, do you have any other customers?"

"Oh … no."

"When was the last time you saw Mrs. Truman alive?"

"Yesterday afternoon, when I cleaned the pool."

"What time was that?"

"Around four, I think."

"She seem okay?"

"What do you mean?"

I turned around and faced him. "She acting any different than usual? She seem like she had anything on her mind?"

"No. She was just sitting there reading a book."

"Sitting where?"

"In a lounge chair by the pool."

"While you were cleaning it?"

"Yeah."

"Was that unusual?"

"Was what unusual?"

"Did she always sit out there while you worked?"

Terry shrugged. "I don't know. Sometimes, I guess."

"Was Mr. Truman usually gone when you worked?"

"Yeah. I didn't see him much. He worked a lot."

"What was Mrs. Truman wearing?"

"Wearing?"

"Yeah, what was she wearing when she was sitting by the pool reading her book? Was it the same thing she was wearing when you found her this morning?"

Terry thought for a second. "Yes," he replied. "I think so."

"How did you get this job?"

"A friend of mine told me about it."

"One of the friends you were studying with last night?"

"Yes."

"This friend got a name?"

"Yeah."

I waited a second. I knew he wasn't bright enough to go ahead and give me the name. I figured that out in the first few questions.

"Is it a secret?" I asked.

"Is what a secret?"

"Your friend's name."

"No. It's Valerie Marrero."

"Who else were you studying with?"

"Lucy Gaffney."

"Who's your favorite Doctor?" I asked.

He quickly glanced down at the TARDIS on his T-shirt and then back at me. "Matt Smith," he answered.

"Always been a Tom Baker man myself."

"He was good."

"Yeah, I guess it's whoever you grew up watching. Had to watch it at five o'clock on Sunday mornings on PBS when I was a kid."

"I watch the old ones on Netflix."

"Oh yeah? I was thinking of looking into that Netflix. You watch a lot of TV, Terry?"

He shrugged his shoulders. "I guess."

"You a Star Trek fan, Terry?"

"Yeah."

"The original series is digitally remastered with updated special effects on MeTV. It looks pretty cool. Crystal clear. You ever catch those when they're on?"

"Yeah, I watch it every week. Can I go now, Detective—"

"Stellar … Jake Stellar."

"Jake Stellar," Terry repeated. "Wasn't that a guy on an old cop show?"

"No, Terry, it wasn't."

Just then a man and woman walked into the room escorted by Officer Pierce. "Jake," he said. "These are the boy's parents; Mr. and Mrs. Blasting."

Mr. Blasting was only about five-seven. He was barrel-chested and slightly bow-legged. What little hair he had was gray and slicked down on his scalp. "Don't ask my son another question, detective," Blasting said. "You can't ask him questions without a lawyer present."

"Actually I can," I informed the bulky little troll.

"Did you inform him of his rights?"

At that point it was obvious that Mr. Blasting had received his law degree from the University of Facebook. "He's not under arrest, Mr. Blasting."

"We were just talking about Star Trek and Dr. Who, Dad," said Terry.

Blasting shot his son a disgusted look. "So then he's free to go?"

"He's free to go," I replied. "But I may have more questions for him at a later time." I glanced over at Terry. "I had a few questions about the Daleks."

Terry smiled and then followed his parents out the door.

Chapter Three

I sat at my desk looking over the crime scene photographs when I heard the door to the squad room open. I glanced over the top of the photograph I was holding as my partner, Detective Avis Lint, walked in. He had called my cell a half-hour earlier to tell me he was on his way in. I told him I had someone coming in to be questioned. He asked me to wait until he got there, so I did.

"Nice of you to join us," I jabbed.

"I left camp the minute I heard the message," Lint replied, sulkily.

Lint had dropped considerable poundage in recent months but was still a porker. He called to mind a pig on roller skates as he made his way over to my desk. "Who is she?" he asked, moving the photos around the desktop with his stubby little index finger, a habit that irritated me to no end.

"Wanda Truman," I answered. "Forty-eight-years-old."

"Drowned?"

"Haven't heard back from the coroner yet."

"Any marks on her?"

"Lump on the back of her head, but it could have happened when she fell. Also a bruise and cut over her eye."

"Married?"

"Yup. John Truman."

"Where was he?"

"Out of town on business … as far as we know."

"Who found her?"

"Kid who mows their lawn and cleans their pool. Terry Blasting."

"Where was he when it happened?"

"Says he was studying with friends."

"On a Friday night?"

"He's kinda nerdy, so maybe."

"He have any priors?"

"Driving under the influence back in June, but that's it."

"So, I'm guessing he walks to work now."

"And everywhere else," I added.

"So, who we got in interrogation?"

"Lucy Gaffney. It was at her house where all the studying took place."

"Shall we go talk to her?" Lint asked.

I stood and motioned for him to lead. "After you."

"Aren't you bringing the crime scene photos in with us?"

"No need at this point."

Lint walked down the hall to interrogation room one. He opened the door and held it for me. "After you," he said.

I walked in. Ms. Gaffney was seated between her lawyer, Blaine Hestor, and her father, Ted Gaffney. I smiled. "Thank you for coming in," I said.

Lucy was seventeen and a senior at North Myrtle, just like Terry Blasting. She had the thick cavewoman eyebrows that were inexplicably popular with girls her age. I tried not to notice that she also had a better than decent figure. Ted Gaffney worked at the motor vehicle department, and Blaine Hestor was a local attorney and douche bag extraordinaire.

"You kept us waiting long enough," said young Lucy. From that point on, I did not like young Lucy.

Her father put his hand on her arm. "Sweetie," he said calmly.

I sat down in a metal folding chair across from them. Lint sat down next to me. We did not apologize for keeping them waiting.

"Do you know Terry Blasting?" I asked.

"Yes," Lucy said with a snotty tone and a look that I wanted to slap off the front of her head.

"Is he your boyfriend?" Lint asked.

Lucy looked like we had just asked her to eat an entire dog turd. "No!"

There was a knock on the door and we all looked up. The door opened and Detective Perkins said, "Jake, there's a call for you. It's Powers."

"Thanks, Perkins," I said, and then looked back at the trio. "It's gonna be a few minutes longer. Please excuse me." I got up and left the room. As I started down the hall I glanced back through the glass panel that separated the hall from the interrogation room. Lint was yawning without covering his mouth and Lucy stared at his giant pork trap in horror. *I should bring him a ham sandwich and make her watch as he eats it*, I thought.

"Hello," I said.

"She drowned," Powers stated. "There was water in her lungs."

"So you're ruling it accidental?"

"No. She had a bruise on her forearm and her index finger on her left hand was fractured."

"Defensive wounds."

"That's what I'm putting in my report. Also the cut on her forehead, as well as a smaller one on the back of her head, contained tiny chips of gray paint— oil based spray paint. It looks like someone hit her with a half to three-quarter inch pipe."

"A pipe that was spray-painted gray?"

"That's what it looks like."

"Any sign of sexual assault?"

"No."

"Thanks, Tommy." I hung up and returned to the interrogation room, grabbing the police report and photographs off my desk as I walked by.

Lint looked at the photos in my hand when I walked back in to the interrogation room. Our eyes made contact. He cocked his head just a bit and I nodded slightly. He knew what my phone call had told me.

I returned to my seat and placed the photos on the table in front of me; blank side up.

"So, how exactly do you know Terry Blasting?" I asked.

"He goes to my school," Lucy answered.

"You're a cheerleader," I stated.

"How do you know that?"

"I did *my* homework this afternoon," I replied. "Terry Blasting seems a little nerdy to me."

"So?"

"So, he doesn't seem like the type of guy you would hang around with."

"What's that supposed—"

Hestor placed his hand on Lucy's shoulder and she stopped. "Detective," he said, "your line of questioning has me wondering why my client is even here at all. You say this involves the death of Wanda

Truman, a woman who was found in her pool this morning, and from what I see in the police report, her death was due to accidental drowning. Also, Miss Gaffney has stated that she doesn't know Mrs. Truman, and in fact has never met her."

"The reason your client is here is because of her relationship with Terry Blasting," I explained. "As far as we know, he's the last person to see the victim alive."

"And he was the *first* person to see her dead," Lint added.

"Lucy's one of two people who can account for his whereabouts during the time Mrs. Truman was murdered," I said.

Lint and I both watched as Lucy Gaffney's eyes widened.

Hestor cocked his head. "Murdered? But I—"

"Some new evidence has surfaced," Lint interrupted. "And it's now a homicide investigation."

"Still," said Hestor, "Lucy has cooperated as much as she possibly can. She has corroborated Mr. Blasting's alibi and has told you all she knows, so unless you feel Miss. Gaffney has committed a crime, we will be leaving now."

Blaine Hestor stood first, followed by Ted Gaffney. As Lucy started to rise from her chair I flipped over the top image of Wanda Truman. It was a head shot revealing the cut over her left eye. Lucy winced and looked away.

"That was uncalled for, detective," said Blaine sternly.

I pulled my business card from my shirt pocket and extended it to Lucy. "If you think of anything that might help Mr. Truman learn the identity of his wife's killer, please, give me a call."

Hestor reached out and snatched the card. He turned and the three left the room, escorted by Detective Perkins. We watched until they disappeared into the squad room.

Lint turned to me and asked, "What do you think?"

"Cheerleaders in my school were bitches," I replied. "And they never spent Friday night with someone like me … or Terry Blasting."

Chapter Four

I was on my cell phone when I pulled into the driveway. I reached up and hit the opener that was clipped to my visor and the over-head door lifted. "When will they be back in town?" I asked.

"Tomorrow evening," Gwen replied.

"So, did the girl say she was with Blasting?"

"I didn't speak with Valerie directly, but her father said, that *she* said, the three of them were studying at the Gaffney's home until after midnight. I asked them to stop by the police station Monday afternoon, after school lets out."

"Okay, Gwen, thanks." I hung up. Bree's car wasn't in the garage. I backed up my truck and moved it over a few feet so she would be able to get by me with her car, and then parked in the driveway. I glanced over at my lawn and noticed it needed to be cut. I wondered how much Terry Blasting would charge me. I looked at the time on my cell. It was four o'clock. I was supposed to pick up Lint at five and head over to John Truman's sister's home, where Truman said he would be staying the night. Truman's sister, Layla Lung, and her husband Ho, lived right down the street from him.

I walked in through the garage and hit the buttons on the key pad that unlocked the doorknob. Keyless entry doorknobs were one of the best investments I ever made. The package said you only needed a Phillip's screwdriver to install them, and the guy at Lowes said even a child could do it, but I hired an adult anyway.

"Woofie!" I called out, as I entered the house. I removed my jacket and hung it on the back of a dining room chair. "Where's Daddy's little Woofinski?"

The next thing I heard were those tiny little toenails as she ran down the hallway. When she slid around the corner I shouted, "There's Daddy's baby!" She was probably a lot more excited to see me than I was to see her, because she's a miniature Yorkie, and I'm a big tough cop.

I dumped out her water dish and replaced it with fresh water while she danced around in a circle on her hind legs. "You want a treat?" I asked. She did.

"Let's go poopy first," I told her. I grabbed the pink leash off the hook next to the door and hooked it to her collar. "Come on."

We walked through the garage and across the driveway into the front yard. I waited as she ran in circles and scratched the ground looking for the perfect place to take a shit. Finally, she found it.

Bree pulled into the driveway and climbed out of the car with a pizza box in her hands. "Hey," she said.

"Hey," I responded.

"I didn't think you would be home this early."

"I have to leave again, just ran home to get something to eat."

The dog was going insane; she wanted Bree to pick her up. I'm only the most important person in the room if Bree isn't home. "You want some pizza, Woofie?" Bree asked jokingly. She looked back at me. "Did you eat?"

"Nope. Just got here."

"Then it's a good thing I got a large pizza."

We went back into the house. I hung the leash back on the hook and Bree placed the pizza box on the countertop. She dropped her keys into her purse instead of hanging them on the hook.

I grabbed two plates out of the cupboard and opened the lid.

"It's got pineapple on it," I complained.

"I like pineapple on it, and I didn't know you would be home."

"So this is the kind of thing that goes on around here when I'm not home?" I took a piece anyway and dropped it on my plate. "We're from New York. We don't like pineapple on our pizza."

"We've been here almost fourteen years. *Now* I like pineapple on pizza."

"You'll probably lose your citizenship."

"Does that mean I'll never get to spend another cold, miserable winter in New York?"

I grabbed a can of ginger ale out of the fridge and carried it, along with my plate, to the table. The dog whined continuously for one of us to drop a piece of our pizza on the floor. If Bree wasn't watching, I would have. Bree thinks the dog shouldn't eat anything but $63 bags of dog food. It's still hard for me to believe the brand is actually called Solid Gold. If that isn't rubbing your nose in it, I don't know what is.

"So, what called you away from breakfast this morning?" Bree asked.

"A lady was found dead in her swimming pool this morning," I answered.

"How old?"

"Forty-eight."

"Married?"

"Yup."

"Murder?"

"Looks that way."

"Got a suspect?"

"Nope, just a high school girl I hate."

"Cheerleader?"

I looked up from my pizza. "How the hell did you know that?"

"You've hated cheerleaders since eighth grade when—"

"I never should have told you that story," I said regretfully. "I didn't think it would come back to haunt me."

"Really? Because you didn't know all women love bringing up the past? Besides, it's a funny story."

"To you maybe, but not to a thirteen-year-old boy with his pants around his ankles."

Bree almost choked on her pizza, laughing.

"Yeah, laugh it up," I said. I shoved the last bite of pizza into my mouth. "I gotta go." I grabbed my jacket off the back of the chair, slipped it on, and adjusted my holster that was clipped to my belt. "I shouldn't be long." I bent over and kissed Bree on the cheek. "Love ya."

"I love you too."

As I walked to my truck I thought about Daniella Ornorato, the cheerleader who embarrassed me in the eighth grade. I hoped she was fat now, on welfare, and lived in a trailer park.

Chapter Five

Lint called me as I was backing out of my driveway to tell me that I should pick him up at Bertie's house. Bertie was Roberta Clodfelter, the woman that Lint had been dating for almost a year now. She was a few years older than Lint and was the widow of a wealthy man who had left her with no worries. Lint was staying at Bertie's more and more as time went by, but hadn't really pulled the trigger on officially moving in. He sounded pretty excited on the phone and said that he had something *really cool*—his words—to show me.

I pulled to the curb in front of Bertie's place. Lint came out the front door seconds later with one of the biggest smiles I had ever seen on his face, including the one he had upon the return of the McRib.

I waved him to the truck and then he waved me up the driveway. I climbed out of the truck and started toward him. Just as I noticed the garage door opener in his hand, he pointed it at the overhead door, and pressed the button. The door rose to reveal the front end of a brand new, white Audi A7.

Bertie stepped through the front door wearing the same grin.

"Who's got the greatest girlfriend in the world?" Lint sang out.

"I'm guessing it's you," I replied, without singing.

"That's right, me. What do you think? It's my birthday present from Bertie."

"Wow! That's really nice, Lint."

Bertie walked up behind Lint and put her arms around him and rested her head on his back fat. "I just wanted to get this big 'ole teddy bear something nice," she cooed.

"When is your birthday?" I asked.

"Three days ago," Lint replied.

"Oh … sorry. I didn't know."

"That's okay, pal. I probably never mentioned it."

"Beautiful car, Bertie," I said. "Come on, Lint, we better get going."

"Let's take the Audi."

"Let's take my truck."

"Come on, let's take her for a ride."

"Okay," I agreed reluctantly. "Bye, Bertie."

"Bye, Jake. Bye, Avis-honey" When she gave Lint a sloppy kiss, I thought he was going to float on air like Snuffles, Quick Draw McGraw's bloodhound, after he'd scarfed down a dog biscuit in those old Hanna-Barbara cartoons.

Lint was grinning from ear to ear as we drove down Ocean Boulevard. He had the window down and his left arm draped over the door. Gordon Lightfoot's *Carefree Highway* played a little too loud on the Sirius radio, but I loved that mellow song at any volume.

"Try to get all that smiling out of your system before we get to where we're going," I said.

The smile promptly left his face. "Was I smiling? Sorry, I've just never had a car this nice before."

I wanted to ask how much Bertie paid, but I also knew I didn't really want to know. Was I jealous? No, I just hate Lint having something I don't.

John Truman's sister lived two houses up from him and across the street. Uniforms had questioned everyone else on the street, but Mr. and Mrs. Lung weren't home at the time. We took a left off Ocean Boulevard onto Thirteenth Avenue. I looked over at the Truman house as we drove by. There was yellow police tape in the shape of an X on the front door, and woven through the wrought iron at both gates.

Lint pulled to the curb. We got out of the car, and as we walked up the Lung's driveway, Lint kept looking over his shoulder at his new ride.

"Knock it off," I said.

"Knock what off?" he shot back.

"Quit staring at the car."

"I can't help it."

"Try real hard." I knocked on the door and reached for my badge. Lint reached for his.

The door opened. John Truman's sister was a mousy woman whose skin tone was that of notebook paper. She was slightly overweight, and her hairstylist must have used bowl number three when giving her the Moe Howard-like haircut. She even had the same hair color as Moe—cow shit brown.

"Mrs. Lung?" I asked.

"Yes," she replied quietly.

I flashed my gold shield. "I'm Detective Jake Stellar, from the North Myrtle Beach Police Department, and this is Detective Avis Lint." Lint flashed his shield as well.

She pulled the door open a little farther. "Please, come in."

"Thank you."

She shut the door behind us and we followed her to the living room. "Please, have a seat. My brother is lying down. I'll let him know you're here."

When she was out of ear shot, Lint whispered, "I wonder if there's an albino Curly and Larry lurking about."

"So, it's not just me?" I replied.

Lint snickered and glanced out the front window at his car.

"Knock it off," I scolded, once again.

He craned his neck like a prairie dog hearing the

click of a photographer's shutter. "There's kids out there with a ball."

"Don't worry about it."

"But they're throwing it."

"What's going on out there?" John Truman asked when he entered the living room.

"Some kids are out there—"

"Good afternoon, Mr. Truman," I interrupted. I extended my hand and we shook. "Sorry for your loss."

"Yeah, sorry for your loss," said Lint, never taking his eyes from the window.

"Thank you," Truman said. "I can't believe this has happened." He sat down in a chair across from the couch, so I sat on the couch. The kids out front finally moved on and Lint took a seat at the opposite end of the couch.

Mrs. Lung stuck her head back in the room. "Can I offer you gentleman a cup of tea?" she asked.

"No thank you," I said. Lint briskly nodded his head no. She turned and left the room.

"Do you have any leads?" Truman asked.

"Not at this time," I replied. "Most of your neighbors have been questioned and none of them saw anything suspicious."

"Can you think of anyone who may have wanted to harm your wife?" Lint asked.

"Harm Wanda? Why would anyone want to harm Wanda?" Truman asked.

"That's what we're trying to find out, Mr. Truman," I said.

"Call me John."

"John, some of the questions we ask may seem strange to you, but we have to ask them. The slightest thing may jog your memory."

"Yeah, I get that, but what I meant was … Wanda wasn't somebody that other people would get angry with. And she rarely became angry with others. She was easy going. She never lost her temper. She is … was one of those people that *other* people always took advantage of, and it never bothered her. It drove *me* crazy sometimes."

"What do you mean?" Lint asked.

"Well, take for example when she had a job, her coworkers always found some way to get her to do their work for them. They always pushed their shit onto her, and she never got any recognition for it."

"And that never made her angry?" Lint asked.

"No. Stressed out, but never angry."

"Where did Wanda work?" I asked.

"She worked at the hospital."

"Was she a nurse?"

"No, she had an administrative position. Public coordinator … something or other. I can't remember the exact title. Something to do with insurance."

"Why did she stop working?" Lint asked.

"When my work took off and my paycheck increased we bought this place and we decided she would stay home. Her job was very stressful, and I thought it would be nice if she could just take it easy."

"How long ago did she leave her job?" Lint asked.

"Seven or eight months ago," Truman answered, almost in the form of a question.

"You're in real estate," I said.

"Yes. Commercial properties. Retail, mostly. The company I work for—Windsor Mall—buys property and builds strip malls."

"And you've been in Charlotte for the last three days?" I asked.

"Yes."

"Why didn't you drive?" Lint asked.

"What do you mean?"

"I mean, it's only a three and a half hour drive," said Lint. "Why did you fly? You could have driven it in a few hours."

"The company pays for it. If *I* had to pay," Truman chuckled, "I would probably have driven."

Lint chuckled as well. It was a fake chuckle. "No wonder everything at the mall is so damn expensive."

"I'll bring that up at the next meeting," Truman said dryly.

"Did your wife enjoy staying home?" I asked.

"She loved it. She decorated our home all by herself. She always had an eye for that kind of thing."

"You do have a lovely home," I said.

Truman nodded and stared at the floor. "I don't know if I'll be able to stay there."

"How long did Terry Blasting work for you?" I asked.

"I don't know, maybe about four or five months."

"Who recommended him to you?"

"Um … I'm not sure. Someone told my wife about him. We discussed it, and she hired him."

"Never any problems with him?" Lint asked.

"No, not at all. I mean, I didn't see him a lot. He was usually here when I was at work. He would come after school and by the time I got home from work he was finished and gone. But the few times I spoke with him he seemed like a nice enough kid. Kinda of a pussy. You know what I mean?"

"No," I replied. "What do you mean?"

"Quiet, kind of dorky, probably never been laid. You know the type. All of a sudden he'll probably turn gay someday."

"Yeah, I know the type," I said.

"Those quiet kids, they're always turning gay," Lint added.

Truman chuckled. "What are you gonna do? Who am I to judge?"

Lint and I shot each other a look. I got up and Lint did the same. "Well, thank you for your time, John." I reached into my inside jacket pocket. "Here's my card. If you think of anything else, please give me a call."

Truman took the card. "I sure will."

"And we'll be in touch."

Lint turned and headed for the door; I followed. Just before we walked outside I turned and did a Columbo. "Oh, just one more thing, John, a few of your neighbors saw you demolish a lawnmower in your front yard awhile back."

All expression left Truman's face. "Yeah?"

"Yeah. They said you seemed pretty angry."

"Did they?" He grinned nervously. "What does that have to do with anything?"

"Do you have a problem with anger, Mr. Truman?" I purposely didn't use his first name. I wanted him to know that I could become unfriendly if need be.

"No. It was just a bad day and the mower wouldn't start."

"I figured it was something like that."

Lint and I walked down the sidewalk and across the street. I walked around to the passenger side of the car and rested my forearms on the roof. "Those not-so-quiet tough guys can all of a sudden lose their temper someday," I told Lint. "You know the type."

"What are ya gonna do?" Lint replied. "Who am I to judge?"

We climbed in. Lint started the car and hit the gas. I think he may have left a tire mark in the neighbor's front yard. I hoped we wouldn't hear about it later.

"You hungry?" Lint asked.

"Not really," I answered. "I had a couple slices of pizza when I stopped home."

Lint glanced down at the clock in the dash. "That was almost two hours ago." He took a right on Eleventh Avenue.

"Believe it or not, I don't eat every two hours."

"Well I'm hungry. You mind if we stop at Sonic?"

"I guess not. What happened to your diet?"

"It's dinner, Jake. Whether I'm on a diet or not, I still have to eat dinner."

"How much have you lost?"

"Fifteen pounds."

"Pretty good," I remarked. But I was thinking, holy shit, that's about how much I've gained in the last few months.

"You seemed to have put on a few pounds there, pal," Lint ribbed. "How much have you gained?"

I gave him the old what-the-fuck-are-ya-talkin'-about look at the exact same moment the subconscious part of my brain sucked in my gut. "I haven't gained anything," I lied.

When the light turned green Lint made a left onto North Kings Highway.

I reached into my pocket for my cell phone and dialed Perkins.

"Hello?" said Perkins.

"Hey, I want you to check out John Truman's whereabouts during the time his wife was murdered. Find out where he stayed when he was in Charlotte. It's only a three and a half hour drive from there to here. If he pushed it he could have made it here and back in six. Check car rentals in the area, see if he rented a car while he was there. If he did, check the mileage."

"You got it."

I hung up just as Lint pulled into Sonic and up to the menu board. "Are you sure you don't want anything?" he asked.

"I'm positive."

He cocked his head and gave me a little duck face.

"Fine! Get me a cheeseburger and fries … and a Coke."

"I knew you were hungry."

"I wasn't hungry."

Welcome to Sonic. Can I take your order?

"Yes, thank you. I'll have a cheeseburger, two chili Coney Dogs, two medium Cokes, and two fries."

The kid read the order back correctly and gave the total.

"So you really haven't gained any weight?" Lint asked.

"Shut up."

Chapter Six

It was dark by the time I got home. I hated this time of the year. Six o'clock is too early for the sun to set. And fifty-one degrees was too damn cold. I remember at home, in the spring—I still called the Bronx home after all these years—we would put on shorts when it hit fifty-one. I climbed out of my truck and went inside. Woofie came running to greet me.

"Where's Mommy?" I asked. I knew she was probably with her friend Aida at the mall. It had been a month since she had purchased her last pair of running shoes, so she was due.

I checked Woofie's water dish; it was full. I went to the fridge for the leftover pizza, even though I wasn't at all hungry. Bree must have eaten the rest of it because there wasn't any in there. It was just as well.

I unclipped my weapon from my belt. I had carried a Smith and Wesson .45 semi-automatic for the past few months, but had recently switched back to my old 9mm because it was lighter. I now kept the .45 in the nightstand drawer next to the bed. I placed my 9mm in the cupboard over the microwave.

"You want a treat, Woofinski?" I asked.

Woofie jumped up on her hind legs and danced around. She let out a couple loud barks. I grabbed the jug of treats off the top of the fridge and tossed one in the air. She shut her eyes and turned her head like a kid who had never been thrown a baseball. I laughed. "You're supposed to catch it, nutsy."

Woofie ate the treat off the floor.

"Five-second rule," I said.

I went into the living room, sat in my recliner and was out like a light.

*****

The slamming of the door startled me awake. The dog jumped off my lap and ran out of the room.

"You home?" Bree called out.

"No," I hollered back.

"Wise ass."

I could hear the unmistakable crinkling sound of plastic clothing store bags as she hurried them down the hall to her closet—that being one of the spare bedrooms where I had installed several shelves and closet rods. Bree had far too many articles of clothing to fit in a conventional closet. Some people collect salt and pepper shakers. Some people collect bells. Some people collect vinyl record albums. I even met a woman once who collected Civil War surgical equipment; she's now serving life in Dannemora. Bree collects clothes. It's not a collection she's proud of, and based on her past reactions when I've brought it up, it's not a collection she wants to discuss. I throw in my jab now and then, but for the most part, I've learned to ignore it.

She dropped the bags in the closet and came into the living room. "What are ya doing?" she asked.

"Watching TV," I replied.

"You hungry?"

"I grabbed something after we interviewed the husband." *Don't ask where*, I was thinking.

"Where did you eat?"

Crap. "We stopped at Sonic."

Bree sat down on the couch. "I'm guessing that was your idea."

"Why would you guess that?" I picked up the remote from the end table and began surfing through the channels.

"Because Bertie told me Avis has lost about twenty pounds."

"Good for Avis."

"You probably shouldn't be eating there and tempting him like that."

"He tempted me. It was his idea, and why shouldn't I be eating there?"

Bree's eyes went instinctively to my belly. "Because I think you've probably gained as much as he's lost in the last few months."

"I have not," I replied defensively. "Besides, I always gain a few pounds during the holidays."

"It's October, Jake. What holidays? It looks like you've gained back everything you lost two years ago."

"I have not." *I had too*. I needed out of this conversation. "So, what did you buy today?" There, that would do it.

She ignored the question and turned her head toward the TV.

"New running shoes?" I asked.

"No," she shot back. "I just got running shoes last month."

"Like that would stop you," I mumbled.

"Really?"

That hit a nerve. Maybe she would let up on the weight speech now. I should have quit then, while she was still in a good mood. But I couldn't. "So, what did you buy?"

"A couple tops."

"Sounded like an awful lot of bags for a couple tops."

"Oh, did it, *Detective* Stellar? I guess you've solved the case of the *too many shopping bags*."

"I would have called it the over-spending caper."

The look she gave me said I had stepped slightly over the line.

"Come on, Woofie," Bree said. "Let's go for a walk."

She got up and walked out of the room. I heard her grab the leash off the hook.

"You want me to come with you?" I called out.

"No," she replied. "Why don't you run to my closet and investigate while I'm gone." The house shook a little when she slammed the door.

I sat there and flipped through the stations until I came to TLC. *My 600-lb Life* was on. I knew I hadn't gained too much weight.

Chapter Seven

I was sitting at my desk in the squad room; not where I wanted to be on a Sunday morning. I had picked up a dozen donuts at Krispy Kreme on my way into the station and had already eaten three of them. Bree had made breakfast when she returned from her run. She offered me some, but I don't eat that shit. Egg whites in a cardboard container looks a little too much like horse semen to me.

I told Lint to be in by ten. I figured there was no reason for him to get there too early. I was still waiting to hear back from Perkins about John Truman's stay in Charlotte, and Valerie Marrero—the other girl in the study group—wasn't due back in town with her parents until late in the day.

The door that led from the squad room to the parking lot opened, and in walked Captain Merle Stein. He was wearing blue jeans—something he only did on the weekends—and a white long-sleeved dress shirt with a button-down collar. His jet black hair was combed straight back. It was October, but Merle had the same dark tan he had in the summer. We all knew he went to a tanning salon, but he wouldn't admit it. Once when Lint brought it up, Merle acted as though he had been accused of visiting a whore house.

"Where we at?" Merle asked.

"I'm sitting here at my desk," I answered. "And you're standing there with that grumpy look on your face."

"It's Sunday," he informed me.

"I know, and yesterday was Saturday and I spent *that* here too."

"I'll put you in for the Medal of Valor. Now what do we got?"

I broke it down quickly. "Dead lady in a pool. Husband away on business. Body found by kid who cuts the lawn. Everyone has an alibi. Husband once murdered a lawnmower."

"Sounds just like a shitty detective novel."

"And I may write it someday."

"Where's Avis?"

"He'll be in shortly."

"Perkins?"

"Making sure the husband was where he said he was for as long as he said he was."

"Gwen?"

"Checking into everyone's past."

"Fantastic." Merle spun on his heels and headed back toward the door. "Keep me posted. See you in the morning."

"Thanks for stopping in," I replied. "Come again."

I walked over to the table that sat under the television, that sat on a shelf, and poured myself a cup of coffee, then I grabbed another glazed donut. I reached up and turned on the TV. It was on ESPN. A soccer game was underway, so I quickly started flipping through the channels to try to find a real sport or anything worth watching. I settled on HLN; Forensic Files was on. I figured if the episode was about a dead lady in a swimming pool I would be home early; it wasn't. However, I had seen the episode before. It was about a man who spent fifteen years in prison for murdering his wife. Turned out, he didn't kill her. I wondered if the guy had ever beaten a lawnmower to death.

Just as I sat back down in my chair and put my feet up, Lint walked through the door. *Damn, he is getting thinner*, I thought. *Still fat, but thinner*. Months earlier I had tried to sabotage his weight loss by systematically placing dishes of candy around the squad room. I ended up eating most of the candy. *What was I going to do?* I wondered. I needed to stop this craziness.

"Morning, Jake," Lint said with a grin. He never grinned pre-Bertie.

"Morning," I replied.

"Where we at?"

"We haven't budged."

"You're liking the husband for this, aren't you?"

"Let's see what Perkins comes back with first."

"I'm leaning toward the kid."

"There's coffee and donuts over there," I said.

Lint poured himself a cup, didn't add sugar or cream, and returned to my desk with no donut in his hand. "This the crime scene report?" he asked, pointing at a folder in front of me.

"Yeah."

He opened the folder and began moving the contents around the desk with his stubby index finger. God, I hated when he did that; he probably knew I hated it "Anything out of the ordinary?"

"Terry Blasting's fingerprints were found inside the house."

"Well, he does work there."

"The print was found on a TV remote control in the master bedroom. They also pulled one of his prints from the refrigerator door handle."

"I knew it," Lint said proudly. "The kid was doin' her. They got in a fight. He hit her in the head with something, and then he dragged her outside and threw her into the pool to make it look like a drowning."

"Autopsy report said she hadn't had sex recently."

"Maybe he used a condom."

"Wasn't found at the scene."

"Maybe he took it with him."

"Maybe, but highly unlikely, unless it was premeditated, and I doubt it was."

"There's no other reason for that kid to be in the master bedroom. I say we have a talk with him."

"I say you're right."

"Want me to call him in?"

"No, let's pay *him* a visit."

"We'll take my car."

"We'll take my truck," I argued.

Lint dangled his keys in front of me. "I'll let you drive," he sang.

"I don't want to," I sang back. I opened my desk drawer and grabbed my weapon, holstered it, and said, "Come on, *partner*."

As we headed for the door, Lint commented, "You never called me partner before."

"Sorry," I replied.

"No, no, I like it. But from now on can you just say 'partner', not '*partner*'?"

"There's a difference?" I got to my truck and opened the driver's side door.

"Yeah, there's a difference. *Partner* sounds like you're being sarcastic."

"*Sorry.*"

Lint cocked his head and stared at me across the truck seat.

"Did I say that wrong too?" I asked.

He didn't answer. He just hoisted his butt up into the seat and fastened his seatbelt.

Chapter Eight

Terry Blasting lived with his mother and father at 605 Thirty-Fifth Street South. Two side-by-side concrete driveways led up to the one-story block home. It was very small and very pink. A For Sale sign in the front yard caught my attention. I parked my truck in front of the house and we got out. I led the way on one of the twin walkways that ended at a concrete patio covered by a gable roof.

"Looks like someone's making a run for it," Lint joked as he pointed at the For Sale sign.

I joined in to humor him. "We better set up some road blocks."

I knocked on the door and reached for my shield. Mrs. Blasting answered. "What do you want?" she asked.

"I'm Detective Jake Stell—"

"I know who you are," Mrs. Blasting snapped. "I

just met you yesterday." She nodded her head toward Lint. "Who's this one?"

"This is Detective Avis Lint, ma'am."

Lint flashed his badge as well as his pearly whites. "I'm his partner."

"So I'll ask again: what do you want?"

"We were wondering if we could come in and ask your son a few questions," I said.

"Are ya gonna read him his *veranda* rights this time?" she asked. She revealed the cigarette she had been holding behind the door and took a long drag. She blew the smoke out of the corner of her mouth. "The boy's got rights, ya know."

"We're not arresting Terry, ma'am," Lint explained. "We just needed to ask him a few more questions."

"Should I call my lawyer?"

"You have one?" I asked.

"Well, no, but I can call one if I have to."

"Ma'am, if you would like to have an attorney present while we ask Terry a few questions, that's your right," I said patiently. "We can set up a time to have him come down to the station, and we can bring him into one of the interrogation rooms for questioning."

"Interrogation room?" she asked.

"Who is it?" someone from inside the house shouted.

"Of course, if he has nothing to hide ..." Lint added.

"He doesn't have nothin' to hide!" Mrs. Blasting shot back. "My Terry's a good boy."

"I'm sure he is, ma'am," I agreed. "May we come in?"

"Who is it!"

Mrs. Blasting spun quickly and shouted, "It's the cops, for Chrissakes!" She pulled the door all the way open. "I guess. Come on in. But wipe your feet. We're tryin' to sell this place."

I stepped inside the door and noticed right away that the carpet she was trying to protect was much filthier than the bottoms of my shoes had ever been. I turned to Lint. "Wipe your feet," I ordered.

We entered at one end of the living room and Mrs. Blasting lead us through to the kitchen, where Mr. Blasting and young Terry were seated. They were right in the middle of Sunday breakfast, something Mrs. Blasting had failed to mention.

Mr. Blasting set his fork down next to his plate and swallowed his mouthful of fried potatoes. "What do you want now?" he asked.

"They want to ask Terry some questions," Mrs. Blasting answered. She leaned up against the stove. "You two have a seat."

Lint was eye-balling a plate of biscuits.

"Can we maybe talk in the living room?" I asked.

Mr. Blasting shrugged. "I guess." He stood, picked up his plate, and headed for the living room.

"Grab your plate and come on, Terry."

Mr. and Mrs. Blasting sat at opposite ends of the sofa with Terry between them. All three balanced a breakfast plate on their knees.

I sat across from them—with the doorway to living room on my right—in an old swivel rocker that was very similar to one my grandmother owned in the late seventies. A far-off memory of Saturday nights spent with my cousins in my grandparents' flashed into my head. We watched shows like *The Love Boat* and *Fantasy Island* until late into night while our parents played cards and hacked up their lungs in the smoke filled dining room. I remembered my cousin and I standing his little brother in the swivel rocker and spinning it around as fast as we could. We had talked him into jumping from the chair to the sofa as it came around. "Jump!" we shouted. He did. He hit the edge of the coffee table and broke his leg. We tried to quiet him and did our best to convince him that he wasn't really hurt that bad. But the X-rays told a different story.

Lint stood to my right, his hands on his hips.

"So how long have you worked for the Trumans?" I asked.

"About five months," Mrs. Blasting said, answering for her son.

"And in all that time did you ever witness Mr. and Mrs. Truman in an argument?"

"No, he didn't," replied Mrs. Blasting.

"Please, Mrs. Blasting, can you let Terry answer the questions?" I requested.

"Oh, sorry."

"No, I never saw them fight," said Terry.

"Did Mrs. Truman ever confide in you about her relationship with *Mr.* Truman?" Lint asked.

"Why would she confide in a seventeen-year-old boy?" Mr. Blasting broke in

"Please, Mr. Blasting," I said.

"Confide," Terry repeated. "Like, told me secrets?"

"Yeah," Lint responded. "Anything about their relationship, or maybe Mr. Truman's temper."

"No."

"Did you ever do work inside the home, Terry?" I asked.

"Um … no. Why?"

"You never fixed anything inside the house? A leaky faucet, perhaps. Or hooked up their cable box, or showed her how to work the TV?"

Terry shook his head. "No. I've taken the garbage out a few times. Does that count?"

"What garbage did you take out?" Lint asked.

"Just the kitchen garbage."

"Terry," I said. "your fingerprints were found on the TV remote control in the master bedroom. Can you explain that?"

Mr. Blasting spun around and slapped Terry in the back of the head. "Were you bangin' that lady, boy?" he shouted.

Terry flinched, catching his jostled breakfast plate before it fell to the floor. "No, Dad! God! I wasn't doing anything."

"You tell the truth, boy!" Mr. Blasting shot back.

"Terry, why would your fingerprints be on the remote?" I asked.

"How do you know they were my fingerprints?" Terry asked.

"You were fingerprinted at your DUI arrest," Lint reminded him.

"Oh," Terry replied.

"So, why were you in the master bedroom, Terry?" I asked.

"I don't remember. I don't think I was."

"No one else has your fingerprints, kid," Lint said.

Terry glanced over at his dad then to his mom. "I don't want to answer any more questions."

"You can answer them here, or at the station, Terry," I explained.

"I didn't do anything," said Terry.

"No one's saying you did anything," I replied. "What were you doing in her bedroom?"

Terry stared down into his breakfast plate. "We just watched TV," he whispered.

"How's that?" Lint asked.

"We just watched TV," Terry repeated.

"Oh my God!" said Mrs. Blasting.

"*When* did you watch television?" I asked.

"After I got done cleaning the pool," said Terry. "I was supposed to mow the lawn, but Wanda—Mrs. Truman—asked me if I wanted to come inside for a drink."

"And then what happened?" Lint asked.

"We went inside. She gave me a beer and she got herself one too."

"Had you ever done this before?" I asked.

Terry shook his head. "No."

"How did you end up upstairs?"

"She told me she had gotten the drawer on the nightstand stuck. She thought it was broken and wondered if I could help her get it unstuck. She said *Mr.* Truman would be angry because he had just bought the bedroom furniture."

"Was this the first time she ever mentioned his anger?"

"No. She said he was pretty mean to her." Terry picked up his plate and handed it to his mother. "I have something I need to give you." We watched as he got up and walked out of the living room. I looked from Blasting to his wife; neither seemed to know what was going on.

I shifted in the uncomfortable chair.

Lint suddenly spun on his heels, his weapon drawn. "Gun!" he shouted.

I leapt up, reaching for my own weapon and

moving forward to place myself between the Blastings and the doorway.

Terry stood with a .38 revolver in his hand and terror on his face.

"Drop the weapon!" Lint shouted.

"I … I …" The boy dropped the weapon on the carpeting.

Lint stepped forward and, keeping his gun trained on Terry, kicked the .38 away. He grabbed Terry by the shoulder, spinning him around and shoving his chest against the wall.

"Don't move, kid," Lint ordered.

Terry was bawling and the tears were streaming down his cheeks. "She asked me to kill him," he sobbed. "She wanted *me* to kill him."

Chapter Nine

Lint sat across from me at one of the picnic tables out front of Duffy Street Seafood Shack. We had ordered our lunch and were drinking our sodas.

"I did not expect that," Lint said.

"Me neither," I agreed.

"Now we have to ask Truman why his wife wanted him dead."

"I'm sure we know why, but he'll say he has no idea."

"You think he smacked her around?"

"Either that, or he has a huge life insurance policy."

"Gwen didn't find any history of domestic violence?" Lint asked.

"None," I replied.

"I find it hard to believe that it got bad enough for her to want him dead without any sign of violence."

"Except for the lawnmower."

"You think he somehow found out she was going to have him killed and he struck first?"

My cell rang before I could answer. "Hello?" It was Perkins.

"Hey, Jake. I just got a call from Cecil Marrero; they're back in town. I asked them if they could come down to the station and answer a few questions. He said any time is good with them."

I looked at the time on my cell phone. It was 1:41. "Have them stop in at four."

"You got it."

"Anything on Truman's time in Charlotte?"

"Just waiting to hear back from the gentleman at Hertz who rented him his car. I'll fill you in when you get back to the station."

"We're grabbing lunch now. Then I'm going to stop home for a minute. Should be back to the station a little after three."

"See ya then," Perkins replied, and hung up. I laid my cell on the table.

"He get anything from Charlotte?" Lint asked.

"He said he'd fill us in when we got back to the station."

"Here you go, gentlemen," the waitress said, as she placed our plates in front of us.

Lint got a hamburger with fries. I got a cheeseburger with fries. I was already planning on telling Bree I had skipped lunch. I remember back before I quit drinking I would lie about what I drank. Now I was starting to do that with food.

"How are you guys on drinks?" the young blonde waitress asked.

"I'll have another," Lint replied.

"Me too," I said. "Thanks"—I glanced at her name tag—"Gina."

She smiled. "Coming right up."

We both watched as she walked away; so did the guys at the table next to us. One of the guys made a comment about her ass, and they both chuckled. The thirty-something comedian who said it looked back over his shoulder at me. He wanted to see how funny we thought he was. I wasn't smiling. I picked up my burger and took a bite.

"So," Lint asked. "you think there's some way Truman could have found out his wife wanted him dead?"

"Who would have told him?"

"Maybe Terry Blasting ran his mouth."

"I could see him bragging if she was giving him sex, but according to him, they had never had sex."

"But he said she promised him sex after he offed her husband."

"Which she probably wouldn't have delivered. I figure she was setting him up. After Truman was killed she was probably going to say that it was all

Terry's idea, and she had nothing to do with it. Make out that he was obsessed with her, or something."

"Stupid kid doesn't realize how lucky he is that *she* ended up dead first."

"You think he would have gone through with it?"

Lint chuckled. "I remember a few older women in the neighborhood that I would have killed for to have sex with when I was a kid."

The young waitress returned with our drinks and set them on the table. "Here ya go, guys," she said.

The loud mouth at the other table said, "Hey, sweet cheeks, how about a couple more beers over here." He pointed down at his empty mug. His buddy laughed.

Gina glanced down at me and then to the moron. "I'll be right there, guys," she said.

"Your tip is counting on it," the other kid said.

I looked back at the three elderly women at the picnic table behind us. The blue hair facing me just shook her head.

I took another bite of my burger and watched as Gina went to the table. "Two more, guys?" she asked.

"You know it, sweet cheeks," the first guy said. "And shake that ass a little more on your way back in if you want a big tip." Gina tuned and hurried to the door.

"Tip, hell," the other guy shouted as he reached under the table and grabbed his crotch. "I'll give her the whole goddamn thing."

Lint slammed his soda down on the table and jumped up. His face was red. He turned and grabbed the kid by the back of the neck. The other guy started to speak and Lint pulled his jacket open just enough to reveal his gun. The guy put up his hands in surrender.

Lint leaned in close to the loud mouth's ear. "Listen, you little piece of shit. I hear one more word out of you while I'm enjoying my lunch and I'll shove my revolver up your ass and use you as a silencer to shoot your bitch ass friend. You got it?"

The tough guy nodded.

"Good," Lint said. "Now, when she comes back out here, you'll both apologize for being such assholes, and then when you leave, make sure there's a fifty dollar tip on the table. Yes?"

"Yes."

"Yes, what?"

"Yes, sir."

Lint turned the guy's head toward the street. "Is that Chevy pickup yours?"

"Yes, sir."

"It's parked too close to the fire hydrant, but I'm going to let you off with a warning."

"Thank you, sir."

"Don't mention it." Lint turned back and sat down. He picked up his soda and took a long drink through the straw. "Ahhh!"

The three ladies behind us started clapping their hands.

Lint nodded to them and smiled.

"You're my hero," I said. "for a second there I thought you were going to ask him if he felt lucky, or that a man's got to know his limitations."

"Sorry," Lint said.

"Don't apologize to me." I looked around the street. "Just be thankful no one was recording it on their cell phone."

Gina returned with the beers.

"Thank you," one of them said.

"And sorry about the way we acted before," added the other.

"Um … that's okay," Gina replied. She shot me a confused look and then went back inside.

"I think you've made a real impact on those boys," I said.

Lint closed his eyes and spoke in a menacing whisper. "If I didn't this time, I will next time."

He looked to me for approval. "Pretty good Clint Eastwood, huh?"

"Eastwood? Hell, I thought you were doing Kiefer Sutherland."

Chapter Ten

I dropped Lint off at his house after lunch and then ran home. I told him to meet me at the station at three thirty.

"What's up?" I said when I walked into the kitchen. Bree was doing dishes. "Yum! What's that smell?" I asked, and then noticed the Crock Pot on the counter. I removed my jacket and draped it over the back of a kitchen chair.

"Making chili for dinner," she replied.

I walked over, lifted the lid, and took a deep breath. "If that tastes half as good as it smells ..."

"There's that left-over pizza in the fridge if you're hungry."

"It's gone," I said. I started down the hall toward the bathroom.

"When did you eat it?" Bree asked.

"I *didn't* eat it. I was going to eat it last night but the box was empty."

"Well, I didn't eat it."

"I don't think the dog can open the refrigerator door." I shut the bathroom door behind me. I could still hear Bree discussing the missing pizza with the dog as I sat there scrolling through emails on my cell phone.

When I returned to the kitchen Bree was pulling the pizza box out of the fridge. She opened it and looked inside.

"You didn't believe me?" I asked.

"There were three pieces in here," she said.

"I don't know what to tell you." I grabbed my jacket and put it back on. Bree set the empty box next to the trash can.

"Are you sure you didn't eat it?" she insisted.

I knew Bree had probably eaten the pizza, or thrown it out and stuck the empty box back in the fridge, but I wasn't going to argue about it. "Maybe I did," I said.

"I figured."

I walked over and kissed her on the cheek.

"Just stop home to poop?" she asked.

"Yup."

"You're the only man I know who can only poop at home."

"I'm sure it's more common than we know. You

know what you might catch, sitting on a public toilet. God only knows what kind of germs might be hiding on Lint's ass, for instance."

"I've asked other woman and all of them say their husbands can go just about anywhere."

I sighed loudly. "Please don't discuss my shit hang-ups with other people."

"Sorry, Jake, that's one of the things that women talk about at work." Bree handed me the empty pizza box.

"Terrific." I leaned in for another kiss. "Love ya."

Bree gave me a smack on the lips. "Love you too. What time you think you'll be home?"

I glanced at my watch. "Probably around six."

"Okay." Bree turned back to the sink. "Let's be careful out there."

"You got it, Sarge."

Chapter Eleven

Lint beat me to the station. I hated to say it, but Bertie was having a fantastic effect on him. Weight loss, punctuality—what was next?

"Cecil Marrero just called," Lint said. "They're on their way."

"Good." I went toward the coffee pot. "Perkins here?"

Lint looked around the room. "He was just here. Must be out at the front desk."

I poured my coffee and took a sip. I cringed. "Jesus! This still from this morning."

"Probably," Lint answered. "You seem to be the only one who drinks it anymore." He flipped the folder that lay on the desk in front of him shut. "You should really switch to decaf, or better yet, just start drinking water instead."

I took another sip of my coffee. "Yeah, I'll take that under advisement, doc."

Officer Janie Schaff stuck her head through the door that led to the front desk. "Jake?"

"Yeah?"

"There's a Cecil Marrero here to see you."

"Send him back," I said.

Lint stood and picked up the case file. A few seconds later a tall, thin, dark complected man walked through the door; a young girl followed him into the squad room.

"Detective Stellar?" the man asked.

I put out my hand. "Yes."

We shook, and he said, "I'm Cecil Marrero." He had a strong Italian accent. "This is my daughter, Valerie."

"This is Detective Avis Lint," I said, motioning toward Lint. "We can talk in here."

I decided to question Valerie in the lounge instead of the interrogation room. I pointed toward the door and Avis walked over and opened it.

Valerie and her father sat on the leather sofa. I sat in one of the two leather chairs directly across from them. Lint stood by the door

"Can we get you anything to drink?" Lint asked. "A soda, or coffee?"

"No, thank you," said Marrero.

"May I have a water, please," Valerie asked.

"Comin' right up," Lint said. He handed me the case folder and left the room.

I crossed my legs and set the folder in my lap.

"So, what can we do for you, detective?" Marrero asked.

I looked at Valerie. Her skin was dark like her fathers. She had long brown hair and dark eyes. She had one deep dimple in her left cheek. Valerie seemed to lack the "my shit don't stink" vibe her friend Lucy projected. "Valerie, have you spoken with Lucy Gaffney or Terry Blasting, either yesterday or today?" I asked.

She nodded her head. "Yes, I spoke with both of them several times today."

"So, you know what's going on."

"Yes. They said that Mrs. Truman had been killed and that Terry was the last person to see her alive. They said that you just wanted to make sure that Terry was with us Friday night."

"Who's *us*?" I asked.

"Lucy and me."

"And was he?"

"Yes. We were studying at Lucy's house."

"What time did Terry leave the Gaffneys' house?"

"Around midnight."

"Were her parents home the whole night?"

"Her dad was there, but he went to bed around nine, I think."

"Where was her mother?"

Lint walked into the room and handed Valerie a bottle of water. "Thank you," she said, and twisted off the top. She took a sip and set the bottle on the coffee table in front of her.

Lint sat in the other chair next to me. He had also gotten a bottle of water for himself.

"Yeah," Valerie repeated. "I think her father went to bed around nine."

"And what about her mother?" I asked again.

Valerie looked to her dad and then back at me. "She doesn't have a mom. Her mom is dead."

I glanced over at Lint and then to the folder in my lap. I opened it and began flipping through the papers. I didn't remember seeing anything about Mrs. Gaffney being deceased.

"How long ago did her mother pass away?" Lint asked.

"A year, maybe," Valerie replied.

Just as I thought, there was nothing in the file so I closed it. "How did she die?" I asked.

"I'm not sure," Valerie said. "I didn't know Lucy then. She and her father moved here after her mother died."

"Do you know where they moved from?" Lint asked.

"Lake City, I think."

"How did you and Lucy become friends with Terry Blasting?" I asked.

Valerie smiled. "You mean how did two popular girls become such good friends with a nerdy guy with *no* friends, like Terry?"

"Yes," I said.

"Terry and I have been friends for years," Valerie explained. "We've been in the same class all the way up from kindergarten. We also went to the same church, and were in Sunday school together."

"How about Lucy?" I asked. "Did she and Terry become friends through you?"

Valerie shook her head. "No. Terry and Lucy had met a few months before she moved here. They both went to the same bereavement group over in Conway."

Lint and I looked at each other, then back at Valerie. I opened my folder once again. "Why was Terry in a bereavement group?"

"His little sister died around the same time as Lucy's mom," said Valerie. "She had leukemia."

I grabbed a pen off the coffee table and made a few notes in my reports, then I looked back up at Valerie and her father. To neither one in particular I asked, "Have you lost a member of your family in the last year or so?"

They both exchanged a confused look and in unison said, "No."

"Just checking."

"Valerie, do you know if Lucy knew Wanda Truman, or had ever met her?" Lint asked.

"Not that I know of, but she could have I guess."

"It was you who got the job for Terry," I said. "Correct?"

"Yes," Valerie responded. "My mom used to work at the hospital with Mrs. Truman—that's how we knew her. She had mentioned to my mother that she was looking for someone to mow their lawn and stuff."

"And stuff," Lint mumbled under her breath.

I shot Lint a look. "Cecil, did your wife ever say if Wanda Truman spoke about her husband at work?"

"Spoke about him?" Cecil asked.

I thought about Bree discussing my shit phobias with the other ladies at work. "You know," I said. "Did she ever say if Wanda Truman complained about her husband?"

"His temper maybe," Lint prompted.

"Not that I recall," Cecil answered.

"Have *you* ever met John Truman?" I asked.

Cecil shook his head. "No, but I can ask my wife about it when she gets home later. She would have been here herself, but she had to work tonight."

I flipped through the reports and my notes for a second and then closed the folder and laid it on the table. "I think that's it for now," I said. I glanced over at Lint. "Detective, did you have any more questions?"

"I don't think so," Lint replied.

I stood. "Thanks for coming in." I reached inside my jacket pocket and pulled out one of my business cards as Cecil and Valerie rose to leave. I handed the card to Cecil. "My cell number is on the card. If you think of anything else give me a call. And if you think about it, go ahead and ask your wife if Wanda Truman ever spoke about her husband with the other women at work."

Cecil quickly glanced at the business card and said, "I sure will."

We shook hands and I thanked them again. Lint walked them out the side door that led from the squad room to the parking lot.

I picked up the folder and brought it to my desk. When Lint returned he said, "Can't be a coincidence. Those two kids meeting at that grief center has to mean something."

"Maybe we had better take a ride over to Conway tomorrow and speak with that counsellor," I said.

"They've got a really good Bojangles on Church Street," Lint commented.

I smiled big … on the inside. *There's the Avis Lint I know and love*, I thought.

Chapter Twelve

I pulled into the driveway at the same time as Bree. Funny how things like that happen. The garage door lifted and Bee drove into the garage. I parked in the driveway.

Bree got out of her car and met me at the driveway. She looked back over her shoulder at the house, and then gave me a hug. "You just getting here?" she asked.

"Yup," I replied.

She kissed me on the cheek. "You weren't already here?"

"Nope."

"Huh." She stood staring at the kitchen window.

"Why do you ask?"

"I don't remember leaving that light on."

Bree was turned away from me, so she didn't see me roll my eyes. "What do you mean?"

"I mean, I'm sure I turned off that light."

"How sure are you?" Instinctively I pushed my wrist against my 9mm.

"Pretty sure."

"*Pretty* sure?"

"Yes, pretty sure."

I sighed. "Wait here."

I walked into the garage and toward the door. I wasn't overly cautious, because I knew she had probably left the light on when she left the house, just like she had eaten the rest of the pizza. I punched the code into the door knob and went inside. Woofie greeted me at the door. I stepped aside and let her run out to Bree. I left the door open and walked into the kitchen. I could hear Bree talking to the dog.

"Did you turn on the kitchen light, Woofie?" she asked. I shook my head.

The entire house smelled like chili. As I made my way from room to room checking all the windows to make sure they were locked I thought about screaming "help me, help me" but only I would think that was funny—well, Woofie might find it hysterical as well.

When I returned to the garage, Bree was leaning against the front of my truck with the dog in her arms. "Everything okay?" she asked.

"No," I replied. "There were pizza-eating zombies running amok in there. Don't worry though, I shot them all."

"Very funny," Bree responded. As she walked past me she grumbled. "I hope you shot them in the head, smart-ass—it's the only way to kill zombies, you know … and husbands."

"That's violent, sweetheart." We went inside and I shut the door behind us. "You also left the bedroom light on."

"I don't think I did."

"I'm pretty sure you did."

"*Pretty* sure?"

"Let's not do this again." I went into the living room and turned on the television and put it on The Weather Channel. I had a hurricane to check on. *Crap!* Jim Cantore was live in Myrtle Beach.

"What are they saying?" Bree shouted from the bedroom.

"It's turning a little east," I hollered back.

"Thank God."

I left the TV on The Weather Channel and went into the kitchen to grab myself a ginger ale. Sitting next to the cans of ginger ale in the fridge were four bottles of water. *Hmm*, I thought. And then I grabbed a water.

Just as I twisted off the cap, Bree entered the room. "Water?" she asked over-surprised.

"Why do you have to question everything out of the ordinary that I do?" I asked.

"Because that's what women do … right after they discuss their husbands poop schedule." She shot me a big grin.

I unclipped my holster from my belt and stuck it in the cupboard over the microwave. "You ever work with a woman named Wanda Truman?" I asked.

"Wanda Truman?" Bree repeated. "The name sounds kind of familiar. Why do you asked?"

"She's the woman who was found in her pool yesterday morning. She used to work at the hospital."

"Was she a nurse?"

"No, she had an administrative position. Just wondered if you had ever heard of her or spoken to her before."

Bree shrugged her shoulders. She opened the fridge and pulled out a package of Delmonico steaks she had purchased at Bi-Lo and set them on a plate. Then she grabbed some steak spice out of the cupboard. "You going to light the grill?" she asked. "Or do you want me to cook these on the stove?"

"I thought we were having chili."

"It's chili with no meat," she replied. "I thought you could cook the steaks and we could have the chili as a side dish."

"I'll light the grill."

I walked through the living room, out the back slider, and onto the patio. The whole way I wondered why anyone would make chili without meat. That's worse than chili with no beans.

I pulled the grill away from the house, something I had forgotten to do on two different occasions. That's why there's a black mark on the siding that I've been promising to paint over for the past three years. In my defense, I painted over it once right after it happened. Who knew there was such a thing as stain-blocking primer? I didn't. I'm a cop, not a contractor. *I should call the guy who put in the doorknobs and have him do it*, I thought.

I turned on the gas and pushed the igniter. The gas lit with a *whoomph*.

"Why did you want to know if I ever spoke with that Truman woman?" Bree asked, when I returned to the kitchen.

"I just wondered if she talked about her husband. We found out today that she had asked the kid who mows their lawn to shoot him."

"Shoot her husband?"

"Yeah."

"Will he come mow our lawn?"

"Wow."

"Too soon?"

"You ever hear the name Agnes Marrero?" I asked.

"No. Who's she?"

"She also works at the hospital. How do you not know anyone who works with you?"

"They don't work *with* me. It's a big hospital with a lot of different departments. I don't know everyone who works there."

I picked up the plate with the steaks, and the seasoning and headed back outside. I set the plate on the side shelf and opened the lid. I grabbed the wire brush that hung from a hook on the side of the grill, and scrubbed the grill for a second before throwing on the steaks. I sprinkled on some of the seasoning, turned down the flame a little, and closed the lid.

Bree walked outside a few seconds later with my bottle of water and set it on the table behind me. "I can ask around about her tomorrow," she volunteered.

"No, that's okay. We're going to head over to the hospital tomorrow and ask some questions."

"Hey, we can have lunch together, if you come around noon."

"Lint will be with me."

"That's okay. He can eat with us."

"I can't imagine someone volunteering to watch him eat."

Bree kicked off her sneakers and went to the edge of the pool to put in her toe. "Cold," she commented.

"Remember when we first came down here? We would have swam on a day like this. People thought we were crazy."

"A day like this used to seem a lot warmer back then."

"We've acclimated."

"Now we can't swim, and we like pineapple on our pizza."

"No, *we* don't pineapple on our pizza. Just you do."

Bree sat down in one of the wrought-iron chairs at the table. "Woofie," she called out. A few seconds later the dog ran through the open slider. Bree slapped her lap a couple of times and said, "Come on!" Woofie jumped up into her lap.

I opened the grill and flipped the steaks. "Oh, that smells good." I sprinkled on some more spice and shut the lid.

"Let me see if I've got this straight, Bree said. "You think the husband was violent so the wife asked someone to kill him, but someone killed her first."

"Something like that."

"You think there's someone out there who was hired to kill her?"

"Maybe."

"Sounds like an Alfred Hitchcock film."

"Are you kidding? Hitchcock films were complex, full of twists and turns. This is more like one of those cookie-cutter Lifetime movies where the husband is always the jerk and the poor little wife is always the saint."

Bree folded her arms across her chest. "I happen to love those movies."

"Oops. Uh, how do you want your steak cooked—burnt to a crisp or bloody as hell?"

"Burnt to a crisp. Like your chances for sex tonight."

Chapter Thirteen

Bree had to be at work by six, so we were up at four thirty. I made us breakfast while she was in the shower. I had suggested we take a shower together, but you know how that goes. I took my shower after she left for work, and then met Lint at the station.

We headed out a little after nine for Conway. Lint had called the guy who ran the bereavement group—Pastor Jim Parks—and arranged for us to meet at ten o'clock. The group met every Wednesday evening at seven o'clock at the Methodist Church on Long Avenue.

It was a thirty-five minute trip to Conway, but when Avis Lint is sitting next to you with his pork trap continuously flapping it seems more like a day and a half. By the time we reached our destination I knew everything he and Bertie did from the time we got off work last night, to the time I arrived at the station that morning. I knew what they ate for dinner.

I knew what shows they recorded. I knew which bachelors got the rose. I knew what time they went to bed. I knew what time they got up, and what they had for breakfast. Half the time I listened to what he was saying and the other half I searched the road side for places to bury his body.

We arrived at the church at five of ten. Lint survived; my weapon never left its holster.

The church was a beautiful colonial red brick building with white trim. The front pediment was supported by four massive columns and covered the brick stairway that led to the front door. A sixty-foot steeple, supporting a large wooden cross, rose above the church. A long, brick, two-story building sat to the rear left of the property and was connected to the church by a series of smaller brick buildings. A horseshoe driveway led to the front of the church and a gigantic, lone Deerhead Oak stood in the front.

I took a left into the driveway and stopped in front of the double doors.

Lint pressed his forehead up against the passenger side window and looked up at the steeple. "You ever go to church, Jake?" he asked.

I opened my door. "Used to," I replied, and climbed out of my truck.

Together we walked up the steps and to the door. I tried the doorknob; it was unlocked, so we went in.

Coming from upstate New York, the interior of the church wasn't what I was used to. There was no cathedral ceiling. There were no massive wooden rafters, and no stained glass windows. The only wood in the chapel that wasn't painted white were the pews.

The walls were sheetrocked and painted antique-white. The twenty-foot ceiling was flat and painted white. The windows were clear glass with open shutters. The room was so bright you almost needed sunglasses.

"Good morning, gentlemen."

Lint and I turned and looked up to the balcony we had just walked under. "Good morning," I returned. "Are you Pastor Parks?"

"That's me," he replied. "I'll be right down."

He turned and disappeared. A few seconds later he reappeared through a doorway at the back of the church. "So, what can I do for you on this glorious day?" he asked.

The pastor already knew who we were, because of Lint's phone call, but we reached for our badges anyway. "I'm Detective Jake Stellar, and this is Detective Avis Lint. We were wondering if we could ask you a few questions."

"Of course. Let's go into my office." He walked past us to the front of the church and we followed. We went up some steps and past the altar through a door. At the end of a hallway, the pastor opened a door, stepped aside, and motioned us in. "Please, have a seat," he said.

Lint and I sat in two red corduroy covered chairs that faced the pastor's desk. Parks took a seat behind his desk.

"Can I offer either one of you gentlemen a cup of coffee?" Parks asked.

"No, thank you," I replied. Lint supplied a customary shake of the head.

"So then, let's proceed with the questioning," Parks said with a slight condescending grin.

I removed Wanda Truman's photograph from the folder and placed it on his desk in front of him. "Do you know this woman?" I asked.

Parks leaned forward and squinted just a bit, and then pulled his glasses from his shirt pocket. He put on the glasses and took another look. "No. She doesn't look familiar. Is she a parishioner?"

"No," I replied. Parks looked confused. Then I pulled out the photos of Terry Blasting and Lucy Gaffney. "Do you recognize either of these two?" I asked.

"Yes." Parks put his index finger on one of the pictures. "This is the Blasting boy—Terry—and the young lady is Lucy Gaffney."

"From where do you know them?" Lint asked.

"They were in a bereavement group I held last year," Parks explained. "Here at the church. Has something happened to them?"

"No, not to them," said Lint. "But the first photograph we showed you is of a woman named Wanda Truman. Have you ever heard that name?"

"Wanda Truman," Parks repeated. "I don't think so."

"Mrs. Truman was found dead in her swimming pool Saturday morning," I said. "She had been struck in the head and either fell or was thrown into the pool.

The last person to see her alive and the first person to see her dead was Terry Blasting."

"Oh my goodness! And Ms. Gaffney?" Parks asked.

"She and another girl—Valerie Marrero—are Terry's alibi," I replied.

"And you're thinking they may have had something to do with the drowning?"

"Murder," Lint corrected.

"Yes, murder," said Parks. "Otherwise you wouldn't be here, would you? Terry Blasting is a good kid. I can't imagine he would have something to do with this."

"How about Lucy Gaffney?" Lint asked.

Parks shrugged. "Admittedly, she is a little high-spirited, but I can't imagine her being involved in something like this. She lost her mother, you know."

"We know," I said.

"And Blasting lost a sister to cancer," said Lint.

"How long were they in your group?" I asked.

"Three or four months, I think. Lucy was here first. She didn't talk much about her mother, and she was very confrontational with the other kids."

"Kids?" I asked.

"Yes, the group was for people eighteen and under," Parks explained. "We hold a different group, for adults, on Monday evenings."

"Do you head that one as well," Lint asked.

"No. Marjorie runs that. Marjorie Clemons."

"Do you know if Ted Gaffney or the Blastings attended the adult group?" I asked.

"I'm not sure about the Blastings," Parks replied. "But Ted Gaffney was in Marjorie's group."

"Would it be possible to speak with Marjorie?" I asked.

Parks glanced up at the wall clock that hung over the door. "She should be here," he said. He hit the speakerphone button on his desk phone and pushed the number four on the keypad. "Marjorie, can you come down to my office for a second?"

We heard Marjorie say she would be right down.

"So, you were saying that Lucy was confrontational with the others in the group," said Lint.

"Yes, at first," Parks answered. "But after Terry joined the group, she seemed to open up more. They made friends very quickly and soon became inseparable. Before I knew it she was participating and letting a lot of her anger go. I would tell her that the only way for her to move on was through forgiveness."

"Forgiveness?" Lint asked. "Who was she supposed to forgive?"

"Hold on a minute, Lint" I interjected. "How did her mother die?"

"She had a heart attack," Parks replied.

"And where did the forgiveness come in?" Lint pressed.

Parks let out a protracted *hmm*. With his elbows on the desk, he put the palms of his hand together and rested his chin on his thumbs. "I remember she was very angry with her father," he said after a long reflection.

"About?" I asked.

"Instead of calling for an ambulance, he decided to drive his wife to the hospital himself. He thought it would save time, I guess. But on the way, they got caught up in traffic and Mrs. Gaffney died before they got to the hospital."

"That's terrible," said Lint.

A woman who appeared to be in her late fifties poked her head into the room. "What do you need, Jim?" she asked.

"Marjorie, these men are detectives from the North Myrtle Beach Police Department."

Marjorie stepped hesitantly into the room. "Is something wrong?"

Lint and I both stood and turned to face her.

"There's been a murder," said Parks. "In North Myrtle."

Marjorie's hand went to her mouth. "Oh, my."

"The detectives are asking about Lucy Gaffney and her father, Ted, and also about Terry Blasting."

"Are they okay?"

"Yes," Lint assured her. "They're fine."

"Do you remember having Ted Gaffney in you bereavement group, Marjorie?" Parks asked.

"Of course," Marjorie replied.

"Pastor Parks tells us that Lucy blamed her father, in part, for her mother's death," I remarked.

"Well, I don't think she really *blamed* him," said Marjorie. "I counseled them together several times, and I think it was more that she was angry with her father for not calling an ambulance. Mrs. Gaffney passed away on the ride to the hospital. I believe they had car trouble, or something."

"I think they got caught in traffic, Marjorie," Parks offered.

"Yes, maybe that's what it was," Marjorie agreed. "Anyway, by the time they stopped counseling, she seemed to be much better. I think making friends with the Blasting boy helped her a lot."

I held up the photograph of Wanda Truman. "Do you recognize this woman?" I asked.

Marjorie shook her head. "No. Beautiful woman." She cringed a little. "She the deceased?"

"Yes," Lint answered.

"Do you believe Ted Gaffney was involved?"

"No, ma'am. Terry was the last person to see her alive and Lucy is his alibi for the evening she was murdered."

"Terry's a good boy," said Marjorie.

"So everyone says," replied Lint.

I turned back to Pastor Parks. "You said Lucy and Terry were very close. Did you ever get the idea that they may have been more than friends?"

Parks smiled. "They never came right out and said so, but I think it would be a safe assumption."

I gave Parks and Marjorie each a business card of their own. "Thanks for taking time to speak with us Pastor," I said. "If you think of anything else, please, give me a call." Parks assured me that he would.

Lint and I walked back through the chapel and out the front door. As we got to the car Lint asked, "Remember in the interrogation room when I asked Lucy if Terry was her boyfriend?"

"Yeah."

"She acted pretty disgusted by the question."

"She sure did."

"It doesn't seem like she would have made that face if she had once dated him."

"No, it doesn't," I agreed.

We climbed in the truck and started down the street.

"Bojangles?" Lint asked.

"Nope."

"Why not?" Lint whined.

"Because I'm having lunch at the hospital with Bree."

"What am I supposed to do?"

"You can have lunch with us."

"I hate being a third wheel. Maybe I'll call Bertie and have her meet us there."

"Maybe you won't."

"Why not?"

"Because we're working, not going on a double date."

"You get to have lunch with Bree."

"She works there. We're going to question Wanda Truman's old boss, and then grab something quick to eat. Stop being such a baby."

"You're a baby," said Lint. He always has the best comebacks.

Chapter Fourteen

We took a left off of Highway-9 and parked in the west parking lot of the McLeod Seacoast Hospital. I texted Bree as we walked toward the building to tell her we were there, asking her to meet us in the cafeteria. She never texted back, but was waiting at a table when we arrived. She smiled and waved when we entered the room; I smiled back.

When I got to the table she gave me a hug and a kiss on the cheek; she did the same to Lint. "How are you, Avis?" she asked.

"Good, Bree," he answered.

"And Bertie?"

"She's good too."

Bree motioned toward the buffet. "Shall we?" she said with a dramatic sweep of her hand.

As we walked through the line and slid our

plastic trays along the cold stainless steel shelf, Bree grabbed herself a pre-made tuna sandwich wrapped in thin white cardboard and plastic wrap and a water. I picked up a mixed meat sub and a pint carton of chocolate milk. I glanced back over my shoulder to see Lint choosing a garden salad. He also grabbed a water.

As usual, I couldn't open the goddamn milk carton and had to use Lint's plastic fork to pry it open. I broke one of the tines and had to get him another fork.

Bree took a bite of her sandwich, swallowed, and then said, "I asked around about that Truman woman."

"I told you not to," I reminded her.

"Yeah, but I figured, what the hell, I'd ask anyway."

Lint chuckled. "McMillan and Wife," he said, and nodded his head toward Bree.

"You want to know what they said?" Bree asked.

"Who's they?" I asked.

"Her coworkers."

I took a bite of my sub. "Sure."

"She's a slut," said Bree.

"Was a slut," Lint corrected.

"Did they say what made her a slut?" I asked.

"Same thing that makes anyone a slut," Bree replied.

"Can you be more specific?"

"I heard that she slept with three different coworkers in one year, and she got caught sleeping with her boss's husband."

"A real people person," Lint commented.

"And who did you hear this from?" I asked.

"A girl who works in the ER with me used to work over at the AA&S Center with her," Bree responded.

"AA&S Center?" I asked.

"Allergy, Asthma, and Sinus."

"This girl got a name?" I glanced over at Lint. He pulled his note pad and pen out of his shirt pocket.

Bree cocked her head to the side. "Why, are you going to question her?"

"If I need to."

"I didn't tell her why I was asking. She didn't even know Wanda Truman was dead."

"I won't mention your name," I assured her. "What's hers?"

"Lydia Sumpter."

Lint jotted down the name and wrote "ER gossip" next to it. I grinned, shoved the last bite of my sub into my mouth, and took the last swig of chocolate milk, which ran out the corners of my mouth and onto my tie.

"Goddammit!" I said. "What was her boss's name, the one whose husband she slept with?"

"Carol Tyne," Bree replied.

Lint bobbed his head and mumbled around a mouthful of salad: Right. That's the woman we have the appointment with."

"Don't mention me to her either," Bree said.

"I won't."

"Carol is who fired her," said Bree.

"Fired her?" Lint said.

"Her husband said she quit," I said.

"Well, from what I heard," said Bree, "they pretty much made her quit."

"We better get going," I said, standing. Come on, Lint." He pocketed his pad and pen and brought his water with him.

"Love you," Bree said.

"Love you too," I returned.

On our way out of the cafeteria Lint glanced over at my tie. "If that were water you wouldn't have that stain," he said.

"Same goes for your underwear," I said.

Chapter Fifteen

Carol Tyne sat behind her desk. Her emerald green cat eye glasses rested at the tip of her long, skinny nose. Her graying black hair was pulled back tightly into a bun. Her elbows were on the desk and her bony fingers were interlocked in front of her chin.

Lint and I sat in two chairs across from her. The way she stared at us as we questioned her made me feel like I was making excuses for the over-due book I had checked out of the elementary school library.

"You said Wanda Truman turned in her resignation on February 12," I stated. She had said that, but I was giving her a chance to tell the real story, or to repeat the rumor Bree had told us.

"That's correct," Carol reiterated.

Lint was jotting in his note pad and then looked up. "So then, she wasn't fired?" he asked.

Carol's eye twitched and her lip quivered. She would not make a very good poker player.

"Wherever did you get that idea?" Carol asked.

Lint pretended to search for the name in his pad. "One of her coworkers stated that she was *let go for sleeping with her boss's husband.*"

Carol's face flushed. "Is it warm in here?" she asked.

"I'm not warm. Are you warm, Jake?"

"I'm good," I replied. "Who was her boss at the time of her resignation?"

Carol reached for a coffee cup that sat to her right and sipped whatever was in it. "I was Wanda's boss."

"Awkward," said Lint.

"Was Mrs. Truman let go?" I asked.

Carol stared downward at the top of her desk. After a few seconds she nodded her head. "That fucking whore," she said through her teeth.

Lint and I looked at each other out of the corners of our eyes. We waited for Carol to regain her composure.

"It wasn't only my husband," she finally said. "She was sleeping with two other married men that I know of."

"They both work here at the hospital?" Lint asked.

"Yes."

"Can you give us their names?" I asked.

"There was Kenny Damos, he was an orderly over in the main building," Carol replied. "And Jack … something. He drives an ambulance." Carol leaned in toward us. "He's no more than twenty-three years old," she added in a scandalous whisper.

"Were both men married?" I asked.

"Yes, although I believe Kenny has since separated from his wife. He had quite the reputation around here himself."

"Regular Peyton Place," Lint commented.

"Where were you between eight and ten Saturday evening," I asked.

Carol looked pissed. "Really?"

I said nothing.

"I was with my husband in Wilmington at a charity function. Several people saw us there. You can ask anyone who attended."

"So, you're still with *your* husband?" Lint asked.

"Of course," Carol answered. "I wasn't about to give up everything I had worked for because of that jack ass's one indiscretion."

Lint grinned.

"We would also like contact information for Mr. Damos and Jack what's-his-name," I said.

"I can have that information sent over to you this afternoon," Carol replied. "Now, if we're finished here, I have a lot of work to do."

We stood and I gave her my card. "My email address is at the bottom," I said. "One other thing. Did Wanda ever discuss her husband?"

"Discuss him?" Carol asked.

"Did she ever talk about him in a negative manner?"

"Did she ever mention if he was abusive, or violent," Lint added.

Carol shook her head. "No, not at all. As a matter of fact she never mentioned her husband at all. Most people wouldn't even know she had a husband unless they asked her."

We thanked Carol Tyne for her time and left.

"Lot more reasons for him to want her dead than for her to want him dead," Lint commented on our way back across the parking lot.

"Looks that way so far," I agreed. "Perkins should have something for us from Charlotte by the time we get back to the station."

"When are we going to inform Truman that his wife wanted him dead?" Lint asked.

"We'll talk to Perkins first."

"Can't wait to see the look on Truman's face."

I looked over and Lint was grinning. "You're evil," I said.

"Probably because I'm so goddamn hungry all the time."

Chapter Sixteen

As we walked from my truck to the station I looked up at the sky and squinted; not one cloud. "Weathermen," I sighed. "Granny's weather beetle on *The Beverly Hillbillies* was more reliable than those SOBs."

Lint chuckled. "Can you imagine having a job where you're wrong half the time and people still listen to you?"

I pulled open the door that lead to the squad room and let Lint walk in first. "You'd make a good weatherman," I commented as he lumbered past.

He shot me a look. "Shut up."

Perkins was sitting at his desk; he was just hanging up his phone. "Anything else from Charlotte?" I asked him.

"Yup," he replied, and looked down at some notes he'd been making. "Truman checked into The

Westin Charlotte hotel at three on Wednesday afternoon. According to security footage, he left the hotel later that evening at five and got into a cab. He rented a car four blocks away at Avis. He returned to the hotel at three o'clock Thursday morning with a tall brunette on his arm. The unidentified brunette left Thursday afternoon around three by herself. Truman left the hotel again on Thursday night around six and didn't return until Saturday at two a.m."

"Was he with the woman when he returned on Saturday?" Lint asked.

"Nope," Perkins replied. "He was all by himself."

"Plenty of time to drive back here, kill his wife, and then return to Charlotte," I noted.

"Yes it was," Perkins agreed. "And I checked with Avis, he put 438 miles on the car before returning it."

"A little less than two hundred from here to there," said Lint.

"What kind of car did he rent?" I asked.

Perkins glanced back down at his notes. "A blue 2016 Taurus."

"Have a couple units talk to his neighbors," I said. "See if any of them remember seeing a car in the area matching that description."

"Will do," said Perkins.

"Great work," I said as I made my way to my desk.

"Thanks," Perkins replied.

"You never say that to me," Lint mumbled.

"Say what?" I asked.

"Great work."

"What does that tell you?"

"That you're a prick."

I laughed. "Hunt up John Truman and get him in here for questioning."

"What reason should I give him?"

"Tell him there's been a development in the case," I responded. "People love to hear that."

Lint sat down at his desk and picked up the phone. "Hey, Perkins, you got Truman's number?"

"Yup," Perkins replied, and read the phone number from his notes.

"Hey," I said.

"What?" Lint responded.

"Great work getting that phone number."

"Up yours," said Lint as he dialed the phone.

*****

I was right, John Truman did love hearing that there was a new development in the case; he was at the station within twenty minutes of Lint's phone call.

We had a uniform escort him into one of the

interrogation rooms and then made him wait for about twenty minutes. The guilty usually become more agitated while waiting than the innocent, but with Truman being a hothead, who knew what to expect.

I opened the door and went in first; I was carrying the case file with me.

I sat down on one of the brown metal folding chairs across from Truman and Lint sat down beside me. In Lint's hand was a small paper bag. Inside the bag was an evidence bag containing the pistol given to us by Terry Blasting.

I tossed the folder on the table in front of me, and Lint placed his paper bag in front of *him*.

"Sorry to have to call you down here like this, Mr. Truman," I said. "I know this is probably the last thing you want to be doing right now."

"That's okay," he said. "Detective Lint said there were some new developments?"

Lint nodded. "Yes." He reached inside the bag and pulled out the revolver. "Do you recognize this pistol, Mr. Truman?"

Truman stared at the .38. "No. Why, should I?"

"Mr. Truman," I said, "this gun was given to Terry Blasting by your wife."

Instant confusion came over Truman's face. "By my wife? Why would my wife give a gun to some kid?"

"Terry told us Wanda gave him the gun and asked him to kill you with it," Lint explained.

Truman leaned slowly back in his chair; he

looked as though he had just had the wind knocked out of him. "I … I don't understand. Why? What do you mean?"

"Just what we said," I returned.

"It's a lie," said Truman. "There's no way." The color had left his face.

"We have no reason to believe he's lying," said Lint.

"Where would Wanda have gotten the gun?" Truman demanded. "We don't own a gun."

"We don't know where she got it, and she didn't tell Terry where she got it," I said.

Truman leaned forward, put his elbows on the table, and rested his face in the palms of his hands.

"Why would she have wanted you dead?" Lint asked.

Truman remained silent.

"Did she know you were having an affair?" I asked.

Truman looked up. "What do you mean?"

"The brunette staying with you at The Westin, in Charlotte," Lint replied.

Truman's first thought was to deny it. "That's ridiculous. I—"

I opened the folder and slid the still from the security camera in front of him. "Don't," I said.

"Where did you get that?" Truman shot back.

It was a stupid question, so I didn't answer it.

"We know she spent Wednesday night with you in your hotel room," I said. "We also know you rented a car from Avis, and we know you left the hotel Thursday evening and didn't return until early Saturday morning."

"We also checked the mileage on your rental," said Lint. "Four-hundred and thirty-eight miles, more than enough to drive back and forth between Charlotte and here."

"Means, motive, and opportunity," I explained.

Truman steepled his fingers and tapped them nervously against his pursed lips. "Motive? What motive?"

"Infidelity," Lint answered.

"Who told you that?" snapped Truman.

"We spoke with her old coworkers at the hospital," I said. "They said she was asked to leave because she was sleeping with her boss's husband. A doctor who she worked with."

"That's a lie."

"We were told there were two others," Lint informed him. "An orderly and an ambulance driver."

"That can't be," Truman said. "She wouldn't do that to me."

Lint and I looked at each other, and then back at Truman. "So you're saying you knew nothing about this," I said.

Truman looked up at the ceiling.

"Why would she ask Terry Blasting to kill you?" I asked.

Truman sighed a rested his forearms on the table. "I don't know."

"Did you ever hit her?" Lint asked.

"No!"

"Insurance money?" I asked.

"No! I mean … I have a policy."

"How much?" Lint inquired.

"Five hundred thousand."

"Sounds like enough," Lint said.

"Was she screwing that kid?" Truman asked quietly.

"Not that we know of," Lint replied.

"What about the brunette?" I asked.

Truman shook his head and stared at the table top. "We work together."

"Do you think Wanda knew about her?" I asked.

"No, she couldn't have. This weekend was the first time."

"What's her name?" Lint asked.

"Can't we leave her out of this?" Truman asked.

"Too late for that," Lint said.

"Marsha Allen," Truman said. "She lives outside of Greensboro. That's why there were so many miles on the car. I drove to her place and back twice. We were together all three days. We went to a few restaurants and a couple bars. I'm sure you can check on all of it."

"We will," I assured him.

We spent another fifteen or twenty minutes asking Truman questions and getting names and addresses of the places him and Marsha had visited. When we finished he just sat there for a second staring at the wall. Finally he asked if he was free to leave. We told him he was, and he left.

Chapter Seventeen

"Woofie!" I hollered when I came through the door. I grabbed the small but ridiculously expensive bag of dry dog food and carried it over to Woofie's dish and filled it. I emptied the bowl of water and refilled it. "Woofie," I said again. I paused and listened.

I didn't hear the usual toenails on ceramic tile, but I did hear something. It sounded like whimpering. I went into the living room and looked on the couch and in my chair. *Where the hell is that dog?* I wondered. *Did Bree let her out and forget to let her back in? No, wait, I left the house last.*

I walked across the living room and slid open the sliding glass door. "You out here, Woofinski?" I called out.

I turned and went down the hall. I opened our bedroom door. "There you are. Did I lock you in here this morning?" I bent down and rubbed her head. "I'm sorry. I bet you're thirsty." I turned and went back down the hall toward the kitchen. I looked back to see if she was following me. She was limping.

"What's the matter with you?" I asked. "Trying to make me feel guilty?" I walked back down the hall, picked her up, and carried her to her water dish. "There you go."

I stood there for a minute and watched her drink some water and eat a few bites of food, then I went into the living room. Woofie followed me in, favoring her front right leg as she walked along. I grabbed the remote off the end table, and turned the TV to The Weather Channel.

I took a seat in my recliner, put up the foot rest, and placed Woofie on my lap. I held Woofie's leg between my thumb and index finger gently rubbing it. I carefully bent the leg back and forth at each joint; it didn't seem to bother her.

I locked my fingers behind my head and reclined the chair.

Jim Cantore stood on the Marshwalk in Murrels Inlet, right in front of The Dead Dog Saloon. He indicated that Petrov was turning back toward land. That was the last thing I remember before drifting off to sleep.

*****

At a little before seven thirty, Bree slammed the door, just like she always does. Woofie didn't jump off my lap.

"Where's Mommy's little baby?" Bree called out. I knew she didn't mean me. I was not looking forward to her seeing the dog limping across the room.

"I'm in here," I replied.

"You're not my little baby," Bree informed me as she entered the living room. "You lying on Daddy's lap?"

Woofie let out a little whimper.

"I think she hurt her leg or something," I said.

"Hurt her leg! What happened?"

"I have no idea. She was limping when I got here." I left out the part about being locked in the bedroom all day. No need to make things worse. I knew she probably jumped off the bed when she heard me come home, and there was a good chance that's how she hurt the leg. If Bree knew that, I would be to blame.

"Come here, baby." Bree picked up the dog. "Which leg?"

"Front right."

She held the dog against her cheek and cooed in baby talk: "Tell Mommy how sweetums got a bad boo-boo."

"Probably jumped off the couch when she heard me come in," I threw in.

"Were you excited to see Daddy?" Bree asked the little Yorkie.

"She usually is," I said.

"Should we take her to see the vet?" Bree asked.

"We'll just keep an eye on her. I moved her leg around a little and it didn't seem to bother her that much."

"Maybe she just bruised her pads."

"Maybe."

Bree kicked off her flip-flops and sat at the end of the couch. She pulled the blanket off the back of the couch, put it over her legs, and set Woofie on her lap.

I stared at the television, watching a bunch of fat guys in the woods. The name of the program was Fat Guys in the Woods. I wondered how long Lint and I would survive in the woods. I wondered how long it would be before these guys got so hungry that they ganged up on the weakest guy and ate him. I wondered how long it would take for Lint to bash me in the head while I slept so that he could eat me. I wondered if it was actually possible to sleep with one eye open.

"I'm hungry," I said.

"Oh yeah?" Bree responded.

"Yeah. Are you?"

"No, Aida and I grabbed something at the mall."

Aida Trentinni was Bree's friend. I liked Aida. It was her husband, Luca I couldn't stand. Luca was a banker and made way more money than God. He was a black belt and part-time instructor in karate, and worked out at the gym four days a week. Luca was a douche.

"Did you bring anything home for me?" I asked.

"No. Sorry."

I paused to watch one of the fat guys roll down a wooded hill with no shirt on. I chuckled. "Did Luca go with you guys?" I asked.

"No," Bree replied. "He had a karate class."

"Of course he did."

Bree shot me a look. "I don't know what it is you don't like about him."

"I don't like *anything* about him."

"He's always so nice to you."

"Really?"

"Yeah, really."

"He always wants me to 'better' myself."

"What makes you think he wants you to better yourself?"

"Because every time he tries to get me to take a karate class, or go to the gym, or take up meditation, or do yoga, he tells me that it's a great way to better myself."

"What's wrong with that?"

"I don't need to be any better!"

Bree cocked her head. "Really? Is this a discussion you want to have?"

"Quiet, woman." I got up from my recliner. "I'm going to make myself something to eat."

"What are you making?"

"I don't know."

"There's still lunch meat in there."

I opened the fridge. "Where?"

"It's right in there."

I moved some things around. I didn't see any lunch meat. "I'll just have peanut butter and jelly," I said.

"If I come in there and find that lunch meat ..."

"What'll happen?" I grumbled to myself. I grabbed the grape jelly off a shelf on the door and set it on the countertop. I grabbed the loaf of bread that lay next to the toaster and removed the tie. I took out four slices of bread, placed them in the toaster, and pushed down the lever. I twisted the bread bag closed and then threw the twist tie in the garbage ... like most men do. *Take that*, I thought.

I buttered all four slices of toast, put peanut butter on two of them, and jelly on the other two, and made two sandwiches. I retrieved a small plate out of the cupboard and stacked the sandwiches on it. I returned to the fridge.

"Where's the chocolate milk you bought?" I asked, as I stared into the fridge.

"Move some things around," Bree called back.

I slid the regular milk aside. "I don't see it."

"Ugh!" Bree walked into the kitchen carrying the dog. "If I find that …"

"Yeah, I know."

Bree's search didn't turn up anything either. "You must have drunk it." She turned and started back toward the living room.

"I had one glass. How long ago did you buy it?"

"I don't know, last week sometime."

I poured myself a glass of regular milk. When I returned to my recliner, I repeated, "I only drank one glass."

"I only had one glass with pizza the other night," Bree informed me.

Sure ya did, I thought, as I made myself comfortable in my recliner.

Woofie was staring at me.

"Mind your own business," I said. I set my plate in my lap, placed the glass of milk on the end table, and reached for the remote; it was gone. Sonofabitch!

Bree was holding the remote. The commercial ended and the screen went black. I watched the TV and waited in horror. The narrator said, "We now return to *"Mother May I Sleep with Danger?"*, here on Lifetime."

Goddammit!

Chapter Eighteen

It was two in the morning when the ringer on my cell phone went off. I was right in the middle of one of those dreams that just seem to keep on going and going. Everything you read about dreams claims that they're only about a minute long, but this particular dream seemed to last forever.

In the dream, Bree and I were lying on the beach. The wind was blowing and it was raining like a bastard. Several times I looked over at Bree and said, "Hey, I'm going to walk down to the water. You want to go in?" Every time I asked she would say, "No, I better keep an eye on our spot."

I would get up off my towel and walk toward the water, but whenever I got to the shoreline there were bodies floating everywhere. The last time this scenario played out—just before I woke up—there was someone holding one of the bodies under the surface of the water. I couldn't tell who it was, or whether it was a man or woman. I turned back toward Bree, and up on the beach, John Truman was standing near an ice cream cart. He asked the teenaged girl who was pushing the cart along if he could get a Choco Taco. She said she was out of them, so Truman began smashing the cart with a two-by-four. Right when I yelled "Hey!" was when my cell phone rang.

Some people might call that a nightmare instead of dream, but I always figure it's my mind trying to tell me something, not scare me.

I fumbled for my phone on the nightstand. "Yeah, what is it?" I grumbled.

"Jake, it's Gwen. We got a situation at the Blastings'. Get here as quick as you can."

I had the phone wedged between my shoulder and ear, and was already pulling my pants on when she hung up. I slid the cell into my back pocket and searched the floor for my socks and T-shirt.

"What's the matter?" Bree asked.

"I gotta go to work," I replied. "Go back to sleep."

Bree sat up, flipped on her lamp, and blinked like a drowsy owl in the harsh light. "You want me to make you some coffee?" she yawned.

"Thanks. I don't have time." I ran around the bed and kissed her on the lips. "I love you."

"I love you too. Be careful."

"I'm always careful," I replied and ran out the door.

*****

I could see lights flashing against the sides of nearby houses before I even rounded the corner from Turner Street onto Thirty-Fifth Avenue. I skidded to a stop across the street from the Blastings' house and jumped out of my truck. There were two patrol cars parked nose to nose on the opposite side of the street. I ran and took cover behind one of the units. Per protocol for a hostage situation with an active shooter, all cops on the scene wore bulletproof vests.

There were two ambulances parked at the corner of Burris Street and Thirty-Fifth Avenue. Several people, some in their pajamas, were being escorted by uniformed officers along the sidewalk toward Burris Street.

Lint parked his car in front of my truck and was at my side less than a minute later. "What's up?" he asked.

"Just got here myself," I replied.

Detective Gwen Lawrence was about thirty feet to our right near another cruiser. She ran to us holding a bull horn. "John Truman's in there. He's got a weapon. A neighbor reported shots fired approximately thirty-five minutes ago. When the first unit arrived, Truman fired a round into the side of the vehicle. The uniforms took cover behind their unit and called for backup. When I got here I started uniforms going door to door. We evacuated the other side of the street, as well as the neighbors on both sides. SWAT is en route."

"How do we know it's Truman?" Lint asked.

Gwen pointed up the street. "Neighbor said she was looking out her window when a man pulled up in *that* car, and went up to the Blastings' door. She said even in the darkness she could see he was carrying a handgun. Car's registered to Jonathan Truman, 203 Thirteenth Avenue North."

I glanced over at the car: it was Truman's BMW all right.

"So that makes two weapons that came from the home of someone who said they had no weapons," Lint commented.

"Crime scene didn't find any weapons in the home," I reminded Lint. I turned to Gwen. "Anything since that last shot was fired?"

"Nothing," Gwen responded. "No sounds, no lights, no movements."

"We got a negotiator coming in?"

"He's forty minutes out."

"Give me that," Lint demanded, impatiently flexing his fingers of his upturned palm at the bullhorn.

Gwen reluctantly handed it to him. "Shouldn't we wait?" she asked.

"I took a class once," Lint replied.

I shook my head, knowing this was probably not the greatest idea. "Don't say anything stupid," I said.

"You know me better than that."

"No, I don't."

"Hey!" Lint shouted into the mouthpiece. The bullhorn let out a loud squeal and we cowered, grabbing our ears.

"You don't have to yell into it," I said.

"Sorry."

"Just speak normal … well, as normal as possible for you."

Lint gave me a look. "John Truman," he said. We waited for some kind of an answer. There wasn't any, so he continued. "John Truman, this is Detective Avis Lint with the North Myrtle Beach Police Department."

The SWAT van pulled to the curb about thirty yards to my left. The back door swung open and Sergeant Floyd Brady was the first to exit, with the half-dozen or so men under his command following close behind. All of them were dressed in military green tactical uniforms with SWAT blazoned in yellow across their armored combat vests. Most of the men carried MP5A3 submachine guns. One man carried a pump-action Remington 870 while another carried a M14 rifle. Sergeant Brady—or Pinky, as we called him—carried only his SIG Sauer P220 at his side.

Pinky walked toward me in that I'm-here-to-fuck-shit-up-old-school way of walking that only him and a few guys in the movies know how to do. There was a lot going on, but I couldn't take my eyes off Pinky. Did I have a little bit of a man crush? Hell yeah, I did. As far as I was concerned, there were three kinds of men in the world: men like Pinky, men who wished they were Pinky, and men who lied and said they didn't.

The other members of the SWAT team scattered and took positions around the perimeter as though their minds were linked to Pinky's like drones in the Borg Collective.

"What do we got, Jake?"

"The perp is a male, John Truman, fifty-two years of age," I said, my voice cracking just a bit when I said perp. Gwen tried her hardest not to grin, but she didn't try hard enough. *Goddammit*. "As far as we know there are three residents being held in the home: two adults—a woman and a man—and one minor, a male, seventeen years of age. Truman is armed with what a neighbor woman described only as a handgun."

"Any contact with the perp?" Pinky asked.

"Not since he fired a round into that unit," I responded, nodding my head toward the patrol car to my left.

"Any movement in the residence?"

"Nothing."

Pinky grabbed the mic that was clipped below his right shoulder. "Hold your positions," he growled. "Negotiator?"

"Thirty minutes out," I said.

"Gimmy that horn," Pinky ordered.

Lint handed it to him without hesitation.

Pinky put the bullhorn to his mouth. "John

Truman, this is Sergeant Floyd Brady with the North Myrtle Beach SWAT team. My cell phone number is 1-843-555-0177. Please contact.me in order to discuss your demands." Pinky handed the bullhorn back to Lint, then he grabbed his cell phone and placed it on the roof of the cruiser.

"Polecat for Sarge," came across Pinky's radio.

Pinky grabbed his mic. "Go ahead, Polecat."

"I've got eyes on the perp and one other male in the south-west corner of the building," said Polecat.

"Roger that, Polecat. Hold your position." Pinky stared at the front living room widow, and through clenched teeth asked, "What do ya wanna do, Jake?"

"I—"

Pinky's cell phone rang. He put it on speaker. "Brady here."

"I want to talk to Detective Stellar," Truman said.

"He's right here. Talk."

"I didn't kill my wife, Stellar!" Truman shouted.

I leaned toward the phone. "I didn't think you did, John," I replied.

"You think I drove back here and killed her."

"We checked with the restaurant in Greensboro, John," I lied. We hadn't heard back from them yet. "They confirmed you were there."

"Did you speak with Marsha?"

"Yes, John."

"You're lying! I called her. She said no one phoned her!" John's voice screamed from the speaker.

I glanced over at Lint and Gwen. Their eyes went from the phone to me, and then back. "Calm down, John," I said. "I thought someone had spoken with her."

"Ask him to let the hostages go," Pinky whispered.

"John, please, you have to let the Blastings go," I pleaded. "They have nothing to do with this. We don't want things to get out of control here. We don't want anyone getting hurt."

"Someone's already hurt," John reminded me. "My wife is dead."

"Let the Blastings come out of there, John."

Pinky keyed his mic. "You still have eyes, Polecat?"

"Affirmative."

"Hold," Pinky whispered.

"This little bastard is going to pay!" John shouted. "He was screwing my wife. He probably killed her."

"Hold," Pinky said.

"Terry didn't kill her, John," I assured him. "Let the boy go."

There was a scream from inside the house, then a gunshot rang out.

"Take the shot!" Pinky hollered. "Take the shot!"

A shot echoed through the night, and then another.

The front door burst open and Mrs. Blasting ran out screaming, flailing her arm in the air. She tripped halfway between the house and us and fell to her knees in the driveway.

"Stay down!" someone shouted.

We drew our weapons

"Hold your fire!" I yelled.

Another shot was fired.

John Truman burst through the door firing his weapon. I heard glass shatter somewhere next to me.

Truman's second shot whizzed past my ear. It ricocheted off the asphalt with a sharp *ping*, just like in the movies. Before he could squeeze off another round, Truman's chest exploded. I flinched as I watched his feet flip out from under him. He hit the driveway on his back. Two SWAT members were at his side in an instant, one rolling him over and putting his knee in his back.

Three men ran inside the house.

Pinky was around the car and headed for the front door. "Get a paramedic in here!" he hollered.

What seemed like minutes was only seconds. I holstered my weapon and started around the cruiser.

"Jake," I heard Lint say.

I turned back. Lint was on his knees holding Gwen in his arms; his shirt was covered in her blood.

A gut wound. *How the hell did the bullet get through her body armor?* I wondered.

Every hair on my body stood on end. I felt as though I stuck my finger in a light socket. I couldn't breathe.

"Help!" I screamed. "Officer down, officer down!"

Chapter Nineteen

I stood in the corridor with my back against the wall. Bree stood next to me. She was already dressed in her scrubs and ready for work by the time she got word about what had happened. We were standing across from a large plate glass window that looked into a waiting room.

Captain Merle Stein sat in one of the chairs in the waiting room, with his legs crossed, and his arms folded across his chest. He stared through the floor like he was trying to see what was going on beneath him.

Dill Perkins sat next to the captain with his head back, and his eyes fixed on some point in the ceiling tile grids.

Lint sat in a chair against the wall adjacent to them; he was reading an old copy of *Field & Stream.*

Five or six uniformed officers stood around the room in small groups quietly talking to each other.

"It's not your fault, Jake," Bree said. She put a hand on my shoulder.

"Of course it's my fault," I argued. "I was the senior detective on site. Everything that happened there was my fault."

Bree turned and put her arms around me. "It's going to be okay," she said. "Our best people are working on them."

I caught movement out of the corner of my eye and looked up. A doctor was walking down the hall toward us. He was dressed in blue scrubs. He was wearing a surgical cap and his mask hung around his neck, under his chin. Surgical slippers covered his shoes.

Bree let go of me and turned. I pushed myself away from the wall. I stared into the doctor's eyes, trying to read his mind.

The doctor slowly shook his head. "I'm sorry," he said. "We did everything we could. There was just too much damage, too much blood loss. He didn't make it."

The feeling of grief and relief came simultaneously. He was talking about Terry Blasting, not Gwen Lawrence.

"Have you told the parents?" I asked. Everyone in the waiting room got to their feet when they saw me speaking to the doctor.

Lint was to the door first. "Is she okay?" he asked.

"She's still in surgery," I said. "The kid didn't make it."

"Goddammit," Lint said.

The word spread quickly through the waiting room and everyone returned to their seats.

"Have the parents been told?" I asked again.

"Yes," said the doctor.

"Where are they?"

He pointed back the way he had come. "Just go right down the hallway to the end, take a left, and then take the second right. There's another waiting room at the end of the hall."

"Thanks," I said. "I'm going to go talk to them," I told Bree. I gave Lint a head nod and he jumped up from his chair. Together we walked down the hallway.

"This really sucks for them," Lint said. "Losing both their kids in less than two years."

"Yup," I agreed.

"Can you imagine how hard that's …" Lint shut up the second he realized what he was saying. "Sorry, Jake, I didn't mean to—"

"That's okay, Avis."

He had stopped because he suddenly remembered that Bree and I had lost a son years earlier. Our son, Ricky, was only six years old when he was killed in a car accident, an accident I caused. It was the reason I climbed inside a Scotch bottle for a few years. It was the reason I don't drink now. And it was the reason we moved from the Bronx to North Myrtle Beach.

When we rounded the corner we saw Mr. and Mrs. Blasting sitting side by side in the chrome and vinyl waiting room chairs; they were holding hands. A red headed woman sat in a neighboring chair; her hand was on Mrs. Blasting's knee. I knew from personal experience that this woman was a member of the hospital staff. It was her job to comfort family members, and to help them with transfer arrangements to the funeral home. In my opinion, she had the worst job in the place.

"Excuse me, Mr. Blasting," I said.

Blasting looked up at me; his eyes were swollen and bloodshot from crying. He had a purple bruise on his right cheek bone. "What do you want, Stellar?" he asked wearily.

"I was wondering if we could have a word with you … privately."

"Now? Do you really think this is the right time for something like this?"

I knew it wasn't. It would never be the right time for something like this, but I had to ask any way. "It'll only take a minute," I assured him.

"It's okay, Sam," his wife whispered.

Blasting leaned over and kissed his wife on the cheek. "I'll be right back, Marge."

"I'll stay with her," said the red head.

We stepped out into the hallway. "Let's make this quick. I just lost my son, for Chrissakes."

"I'm very sorry for your loss," I said probably too robotically, knowing how hollow that phrase always sounded.

Blasting took a deep breath and exhaled. "How's the detective?" he asked.

"She's still in surgery," said Lint.

"Bullet to the abdomen," I added. "Doc said it's touch and go."

"And Truman?"

"DOA."

"What happened in there?" I asked.

"My wife woke me up; she said she heard someone at the door. I opened the front door and Truman shoved a gun in my face. He told me to take him to Terry's room. I lied; I told him Terry was staying at a friend's house. He didn't believe me. I asked him what he wanted with Terry. I didn't recognize him at first. He was drunk and slurring his words. He looked like he could barely stand up. I looked behind me and saw Margie standing in the hall. I told her to go back in the bedroom and lock the door. That's when Truman hit me with the gun. I fell down and he grabbed me by the back of my shirt. He was dragging me down the hall shouting Terry's name. He kicked open Terry's bedroom door. Terry had his window open and his curtain pulled back; he was trying to go out through the window. Truman said, 'You go out that window and I put a bullet through your father's head.'" Blasting paused. "He should have kept going."

"Then what happened?" Lint asked.

"He was pointing the gun at Terry the whole time. He was shouting at Terry, trying to get him to admit that he had slept with Mrs. Truman, and that he had killed her. Terry was crying. He kept telling Blasting that nothing had happened between them, and that he didn't kill her. He told Truman that Mrs. Truman wanted him dead, but that he wasn't going to do it. Truman didn't believe anything Terry said. He kept saying that if Terry admitted everything that he would let him live."

"But Terry never admitted it," I said.

Blasting shook his head. "No. Then Truman saw the cop in the tree in the backyard. That's when he shot Terry."

"I'm sorry," I said. I knew I had already said it, but it just came out. "Give Mrs. Blasting our condolences."

Blasting turned and went back into the waiting room.

"Two prime suspects," Lint commented. "And they both went to their graves denying they killed her."

"Yeah," I replied, turned, and went back down the corridor.

When Lint and I returned to the group at the other waiting room, a different doctor was there. I couldn't tell right away by the expression on his face if it was good news or bad, so I made eye contact with Bree; her smile said it all.

"She's going to be okay, Jake," Bree said. "She's out of surgery and they've moved her to intensive care."

I breathed a sigh of relief.

The doctor nodded to me as he turned and walked out of the room.

"Thank, God," said Merle.

Two of the uniformed officers did a high five. "She's a tough one," one of them said.

Bree and I hugged. Lint slapped me on the back. "I knew she would make it," he said.

Merle looked at his watch. "Perkins, Gwen's parents are arriving from Denver at noon. You be at the gate waiting for them."

"You got it," Perkins replied. He stood and left the room. He grinned big on his way by me.

"Let's get some breakfast," Lint said. "I'm starving."

"Go figure," I replied.

As we all walked down the hallway I saw the Blastings round the corner. The red head was walking between them. They didn't look up. There would be nothing for *them* to celebrate.

Chapter Twenty

Lint and I had spent most of the day Wednesday over in Greensboro speaking with John Truman's girlfriend. She backed up his alibi. She said she was with him all of Friday evening into Saturday morning. We spoke with—and showed their pictures to—wait staff at the restaurants where they said they had eaten. They were remembered at each place. The case was at a bit of a standstill.

It was Thursday around lunch time when Bree called me from the hospital to tell me that Gwen was moved from the ICU to her own room.

"That's great," I said.

"What's great?" Lint asked. He was sitting next to me in the new unmarked Dodge Charger the department had purchased a few months earlier. We were on our way to an unrelated case we had picked up earlier in the morning. "What's going on?" he repeated.

"Shush," I said.

"Me?" Bree asked.

"No, not you. This nosy bastard next to me," I replied. "Can she have visitors?"

"Yes. Visiting hours are from nine to noon, and then from three to six."

"Can we go see her?" Lint asked.

I shot him a look. "Are you going down to see her?"

"Is who going to see her?" Lint asked.

"Jesus Christ, shut up!"

"Yes," Bree answered. "I'm going down right after I finish my lunch."

"Okay. Tell her I'll stop in around three."

"Tell her I'll be there too," Lint said.

"Tell her Lint can't make it," I said, and then hung up.

"What the hell did you say that for?' Lint asked.

"What?"

"Why'd you say I couldn't make it?"

"Oh, sorry. Were you going to be able to make it?"

"I said I was."

"I didn't hear you. You gotta speak up next time." I flashed him a grin.

"You're a dick."

I turned right off of Twenty-Seventh Avenue North onto Ships Wheel Drive.

"I think in all the years I've lived here, I've only been over here two or three times," I commented.

"I've been over here a bunch of times," Lint said. He pointed to the first house on the left. "My in-laws used to live right there."

"Nice place. Which in-laws?"

"In-laws number three."

"They still live there?"

"Don't know. Don't give a rat's ass."

We pulled to the curb in front of 2812 Ships Wheel Drive; it was the last house on the right before the turn around.

"So, what are these people's names?" I asked.

Lint pulled out his notepad. "Carlton and Amy Moon."

We walked up the concrete driveway of the split-level brick house, and onto the sidewalk that led to the front door. I knocked, and then we both reached for our shields.

The door opened and I started to speak. "Good morning …" I paused and then looked down at the three-foot woman standing before me and began again. "Good morning. I'm Detective Jake Stellar, with the North Myrtle Beach Police Department, and this is Detective Avis Lint."

"Good morning," the woman replied in a disgusted tone. It was obvious she was angry, but not angry with us. She pulled the door open the rest of the way. "Please, come inside."

We stepped inside and she pushed the door closed behind us. "Are you Mrs. Moon?" I asked.

"Yes," she replied. "Amy Moon. Follow me."

I watched her sway from side to side as she made her way across the beige Berber carpeting of the living room on her short crooked legs. We followed her from the living room into the dining room. She yanked open a sliding glass door that lead to the backyard and hollered, "Carl! The cops are here!" She looked over her shoulder and up at me. "He's out there burying Mittens."

"Your cat?" I guessed.

"Yes."

"Carl!" she yelled again, and then pointed at the dining room table. "He ain't got his hearing aids in. They're both layin' over there. Stone-deaf, stone-deaf."

"What!" Carl shouted back.

"We can walk out there and talk to him," Lint suggested.

"You do that," said Amy. "And I'll make some coffee."

Lint and I stepped through the glass door. The Moons' backyard was like a forest. There were cedar, bald cypress, and hemlock trees everywhere. The ground was a continuous carpet of pine needles. Carlton Moon stood in the far south-west corner of the property. The tall, thin, dark-haired man was digging a hole with a pointed shovel. Next to him, on the ground, was his dead cat wrapped in a beach towel.

"Carlton Moon," I said when we were close enough for a stone-deaf man to hear us.

Carlton was startled and spun around. "What?" he asked.

"I'm Detective Stellar and this Detective Lint. We're here about—"

"The asshole that threatened me, then kilt my damn cat."

"Yes," I said.

Carlton rested the shovel against the trunk of a cedar, bent down, and gently picked up the beach towel. He placed it at the bottom of the two-foot-deep hole. "See ya on the other side, Mittens," he said, his voice cracking a bit. And then he filled in the hole.

"So, you have an idea who might have done this?" Lint asked.

"Idea, shit," Carlton said. "I know zackly who done it. It was that Jesse Bowie, lives over at the end uh LD Drive."

"What makes you think it was him?" I asked.

"I just know."

"Do you have any proof?" Lint asked.

"Don't need no proof. It was him." Carlton picked up the shovel and looked down at the mound of fresh dirt. "Think cats need sumpin' said over 'em?"

Lint shrugged. "Maybe."

Carlton headed toward a shed at the other side of the yard. "Aw, shit, I'll have Maw come out here an' say a prayer later. I never was much fer religion."

"Would you like us to go over and talk with this, Bowie?" Lint asked.

"I di'n't want ya to do anything. It was Maw that called ya. I told 'er I'd handle it myself."

"Nothing good comes from handling things like this yourself," I said.

"All depends," said Carlton.

"All depends on what?" Lint asked.

"If the person handlin' it gets caught."

"Well, that's probably not something you want to say to the cops," Lint said. We looked at each other and grinned.

"What exactly has he done that makes you think he killed your cat?" I asked.

"He's a bastard and a hot-head," Carlton replied.

"A lot of people are hot-heads and bastards, Carlton," I told him. "But that doesn't necessarily mean they would kill a cat."

"He threatened me once," Carlton said. "I walked over yonder" —Carlton pointed in the direction of a wooded area across the street from his house— "a few months ago, 'cause I heard gunshots in the woods. Bowie and one uh his cousins, Zeke, was huntin' over there. I telled 'em to get outta there or I was gonna call the cops. They pointed their shotguns at me and said, 'Mebbe you better get outta here or someone's gonna be callin' a hearse.'"

"Sounds like a threat to me," Lint said. "What did you do?"

"I high-tailed it outta there."

"That what he killed your cat with?" Lint asked. "A shotgun?"

"Nope. Weren't no shotgun," Carlton said. "Boy's got an old Winchester .33 his grampa gave him. That's what he shot our Mittens with."

"How do you know it was a .33?" Lint asked.

Carlton pointed at the back of the house near the sliding glass door. "That hole told me so." There was a small hole to the left of the door, about twelve inches up from the ground. "He missed with the first shot. Coulda come right through that winder and got me or Maw."

Lint walked over to the house, pulled his pocket knife out, and knelt down next to the hole. He pulled a small evidence bag from his inside jacket pocket and held it beneath the bullet hole, and with the point of his knife he pried the lead from its resting place.

"Anything else we should know before we head over there?" I asked.

"He also called Maw an Oompa Loompa once."

Lint quickly turned his head away so Carlton didn't see his grin.

"Sounds like a real prick," I said.

"She di'n't pay him no never mind, she'd heard

worst. She's a tough little thing. Killin' that cat though, that broke her heart. I'm gonna get 'im fer that."

"Mr. Moon," I said, "you just let us handle this."

"There's no need for you to be getting yourself in any trouble," Lint added.

"He'll just say he di'n't do it," said Carlton. "Dem boys need some backwoods justice."

"You just take care of Mrs. Moon," I told him. "And let us take care of the justice dealing."

We left the Moons' hoping we had gotten through to Carlton, and headed over to the Bowie residence.

Chapter Twenty-One

We drove the Charger back down Twenty-Seventh Avenue and took a left onto LD Drive. LD Drive ran almost parallel to Twenty-Seventh and right after making the turn we were headed back in the same direction. The road wasn't much wider than one lane and we soon came upon a sign that read DEAD END. There was a dog kennel on the right that was housed in a building that looked as though it was once a motel.

Right after the kennel was a ranch-style brick house. The blacktop ended at their driveway and became a dirt road. Soon after that we saw a telephone pole with a private property sign nailed to it, and next to the pole were four old mailboxes, each sitting on their own decrepit post.

"I've never been back *here* before," Lint commented.

"Me neither," I replied.

We traveled another hundred yards before entering a wooded area. Another hundred yards after that, we came to the end of the road. We climbed out of the car and looked around. It was a little tornado-bait village. There was a mobile home to our right propped up on cement blocks; the roof was about to cave in from the ton of pine straw and fallen limbs it supported. Two more trailers, which by the forsaken looks of them might house hillbilly cannibals, squatted in mildew-covered splendor on our left. Sitting in front of the trailer on the far left were two sawhorses, some newly purchased treated lumber, a circular saw plugged into an extension cord that ran through the front door, and a few other hand tools lying about. *Well*, I thought, *at least one of the hillbilly cannibals is doing something to promote rural renewal.*

A small, single-story wood frame shack sat directly in front of us. If my calculations were correct, the Moons' house couldn't have been more than another two hundred yards behind the shack.

"What door should we knock on first?" Lint asked.

I looked at each place. There was a big Rottweiler tied to the front deck of one of the trailers on the left. The dog didn't look too ferocious, but he had teeth, so why take the chance.

I pointed at the old shack. "We'll start with that one," I said.

"After you," said Lint.

I proceeded to the front door. "Thanks."

I stepped cautiously onto the front porch, the

tongue-and-grooved floor boards creaked beneath me. There was a small hole I had to straddle. I glanced up at the roof that didn't seem to be supported very well. One of the posts was missing and had been replaced with a two-by-four with one end jammed into the dirt and the other end wedged into the soffit. I knocked on the door. I looked back over my shoulder at Lint, then at the old mutt, and then wrapped on the old wooden door again.

"Can I help you?" came an ancient raspy voice from the trailer on the right.

An old lady stood on the deck of the trailer. A cigarette dangled from the corner of her wrinkled mouth. A black cat sat on the railing next to her. She stroked the cat as she waited for an answer.

"Holy shit," Lint whispered. "Remember to leave a trail of bread crumbs so we can find our way back."

"We're detectives from the North Myrtle Beach Police Department," I informed her. "We're looking for Jesse Bowie."

"You got badges?" she asked.

We pulled them out, flashed them, and returned them to our pockets.

"Whatcha want him for?" she asked.

"We just need to ask him a few questions," Lint responded.

"'Bout what?"

"Does he live here, ma'am?" I asked.

"Yup."

"Is he home?"

"Nope."

"Do you know when he'll be home?"

"Nope, but I'll ask." The old woman turned, opened the trailer door, and looked inside. "Jesse, these boys wanna know when you'll be home."

We could hear someone shout back from inside. "Tell 'em I'll be home around four, Gramma. I got a bunch of shit to do today."

Lint and I looked at each other. Lint shook his head.

"You believe this?" I said.

"Yup," Lint replied.

"Is Jesse Bowie in there, ma'am?" I asked.

"Yup," she replied.

"Why didn't you tell us that in the first place?" said Lint.

"You didn't ask," the old bat shot back, and then let out a cackle to be envied by every witch in the coven. "Y'all asked if he was home. This ain't his home, that is."

Lint and I walked toward the trailer. "Can we speak to Jesse?" Lint asked.

"You wanna talk to these boys, Jesse?" she called out over her shoulder.

"I said I'd be home at four, goddammit!" Jesse shouted back.

Lint gazed into the sky for a second and then

wiped the sweat from his brow. "It's too hot for this today" he whispered. He didn't have the patience I did. He pointed his finger at the blue-hair. "You tell that boy to get his ass out here right now!" Lint shouted. "Or I'm coming in there and dragging him out by his heels!"

"You done gone and pissed 'em off now, Jesse," Gramma said. "You might as well come on out and talk to 'em before things get outta hand."

"Aw, Gramma," we heard Jesse grumble, then what sounded like a chair being thrown. A few seconds later Jesse stood at the door pulling a white wife-beater on over his head. After his shirt was on he left one arm dangling at his side while moving the other behind the doorjamb out of sight.

"Can you step out onto the deck, Jesse?" I requested.

Jesse grinned. "I'm good right here. What is it y'all want?"

"We had a complaint from one of your neighbors," said Lint.

Jesse looked past us. "You turn in a complaint against me, Zeke?"

We turned our heads. A tall skinny blond kid stood about twenty-five yards behind us. He held a double-barreled .12 gauge shotgun, with the butt under his armpit and the barrel over his forearm.

Lint cautiously moved his hand toward his weapon.

"I wouldn't do that if I was you," came another voice from the front porch of the shack. "You keep those hands where I can see 'em."

The man on the porch was older, maybe fifty. He had long gray hair pulled back in a pony-tail. He was as tall as Zeke, and had a patch over his left eye. In his left hand he held a bolt-action Winchester 30.06. In his right hand he held a cell phone.

"Let's not do anything stupid," I said.

"Looks like you two already done something stupid," said Patch. "Ya come on my land uninvited, and without a warrant—I'm 'soomin ya don't have a warrant. Then ya threaten my boy with bodily harm. This is Amer'ca, son. Ain't how we do things here."

"No one threatened your boy," I said.

"I got it all right here on my cellular *dee*-vice. Fat boy there said, 'You get yer ass outta that trailer, boy, or I'll come in there and drag ya out by the feet.'"

"By the heels," Lint corrected. "I said I'd drag that little bastard out of there by his heels."

Patch grinned. "So, you got a warrant?"

"No," I replied.

"Then there'll be no heel-draggin' today. Now climb back in your fancy car that me and the other tax payers bought for ya, and head on back down the road."

I motioned for Lint to return to the car. He gave me a defiant look. I widened my eyes and he turned toward the Charger. Once he was in the passenger seat I walked backwards to the vehicle and climbed in. I backed down the road toward Twenty-Seventh Avenue. Just before we rounded the bend, the Bowies began hootin' and hollerin'.

"Sons-a-bitches," Lint said.

Chapter Twenty-Two

I sat on the dark leather sofa across from Captain Stein's desk. I had my legs crossed and my head back with my eyes closed.

Lint stood in the doorway with his fists on his hips. "What do you mean there's nothing we can do about it?" he asked. "We're the cops, for Chrissakes."

"Did you witness anyone breaking the law?" Merle asked.

"They had guns," Lint said.

"Did they point them at you?"

"No."

"Did they threaten you in any way?"

"No."

"Do you even know if the guns were loaded?"

"No," Lint repeated. "We just wanted to talk to the little bastard."

"But *he* didn't want to talk to *you*. And that's his right."

"This is bullshit. Back in the old days we would have gone back there with a few more guys and shoved those rifles up their asses."

Lint was a few years older than me, so by "the old days", he meant the early 1980s—back before cell phones, Facebook, and YouTube.

Calm down," Merle said. "You know the law. He doesn't have to speak to us and you can't step on that property again unless there's a crime being committed."

"This is bullshit!"

"I know, you already said that," Merle said as he shuffled some papers around on his desk. "Now, where are we on the Truman case?"

It was quiet for a second so I opened my eyes. They were both staring at me. "You're asking me?"

"Yeah," said Merle.

"Same place we were three days ago," I said.

"You're saying we're at a standstill?"

"No. Just a lull."

"A lull?" Merle replied. "A lull is kind of a stand still."

"Not *this* lull," I assured him.

"Let's hope not. I want this case closed soon."

We left Merle's office and returned to our desks.

"I hate lulls," Lint said.

"Yeah," I replied.

"Lunch might help us mull over this lull," Lint suggested.

"Good idea," I said. "Then we'll stop over to the hospital and see Gwen."

"Hospitals, you know, can be rather dull," Lint singsonged. "The poor lass is likely bored out of her skull."

"That's enough, Dr, Seuss." I opened my desk drawer and retrieved my weapon, Lint did the same. As we walked toward the door I looked over at Lint. The expression on his face told me that his mind was elsewhere. "What is it?" I asked.

"I was trying to come up with a way to use cull and gull in a sentence."

"Of course you were."

*****

It was Lint's turn to choose, so of course we had lunch at Sonic. After that we drove over to the hospital to check on Gwen.

The door to Gwen's hospital room was open, so we went in. Perkins was standing beside her bed; he was holding her hand. When he heard us enter he quickly let go and stepped back from the bed.

Perkins and Gwen had been secretly seeing each other for months. The only secret about the relationship was them not knowing that we all already knew … well, everyone but Merle, but he suspected.

"There she is," I said. "North Myrtle Beach's newest Purple Heart recipient."

"Hi, guys," Gwen said embarrassedly.

"We're not interrupting anything, are we?" Lint jabbed.

"What No!" Gwen replied with feigned confusion.

"Good," Lint said. "Then get your lazy ass out of that bed and get back to work."

"You were out for almost six months, Lint," Perkins shot back.

"I got an infection."

"In his brain," I added.

Gwen laughed, winced, and grabbed her abdomen. "Don't make me laugh, dammit."

"So, how did you get shot in the stomach while wearing your vest?" I asked.

"The bullet came through the cruiser's window, hit me in the hip bone, and ricocheted up into my abdomen."

"Talk about a magic bullet," Lint said. "A lot of damage?"

"Enough for six hours in surgery," Gwen replied.

"You ain't shittin' in a bag, are you?" Lint asked.

"Jesus Christ, Lint," Perkins said. "What's the matter with you?"

"Why, is she?"

"No," Gwen replied. "I'm not."

"Well, that's a good thing. I have a buddy over in Loris who—"

"That's enough, Lint," I said.

Lint shrugged. "Whatever."

"So, how's the case coming along?" Gwen asked.

"We're at a lull," said Lint.

""A lull?" asked Perkins.

"A standstill," I replied.

"Two prime suspects, and they're both dead," Gwen commented. "Where do we go from here?"

"Truman had an alibi," I told Gwen. "We checked it out. He was in Greensboro. Several people identified him from his photograph."

"The Blasting kid had an alibi too," said Lint.

"And no other suspects," Perkins added.

"I do not like standstills and lulls," recited Lint, as Gwen and Perkins gaped at him. "I do not like them with a gull—"

"Lint," I said, doing a slow burn, "your poetic license has been revoked."

Chapter Twenty-Three

Bree and I ate dinner at Bimini's Oyster Bar & Seafood Cafe. I had the crab cake dinner. Bree ordered the chicken breast. It was her idea to go to a seafood place. She says she loves Bimini's, but the only seafood she ever orders is fried haddock, and even that's not very often. We both had two margaritas; hers was frozen, mine was on the rocks and virgin.

It was dark by the time we left the restaurant. I took a right onto North Kings Highway. Bree's cell phone rang; it was a woman she works with asking her if she would switch shifts with her. Bree said "of course." They spoke for about a minute more and Bree hung up.

"We weren't doing anything Friday night, were we?" Bree asked.

"Not that I know of," I answered.

"Good, because I switched Thursday for Friday."

"Okay," I said, knowing I would never remember she told me that.

I usually made a right-hand turn onto Twenty-Seventh Avenue if we were on our way home from the south, but I drove on by.

"Where are we going?" Bree asked.

"Just taking a little ride," I answered.

"You missed my street, mister," she joked. "Where are you taking me?"

"I feel like I'm the neighborhood pervert in an *ABC After School Special*," I said.

I turned onto Sixteenth Avenue and slowed to about twenty miles per hour.

"Will you take me for ice cream, mister?" Bree asked innocently.

I slowed at each intersection even if there wasn't a stop sign, and looked both ways.

"Sure, young lady, I'll take you for ice cream," I replied with a lecherous laugh.

We got to Holly Drive and I made a left.

Bree pulled up the console between us and slid over next to me. She placed her hand on my inner thigh and squeezed. "I would do just about anything for a peanut butter sundae."

Well, this doesn't happen often, I thought.

I drove another two blocks, and sitting next to a steel dumpster was just what I was looking for; a shopping cart. I pulled my truck to the side of the street. "Hold that thought," I said, and climbed out of the truck. I walked to the back of my truck and opened the tailgate. I picked up the shopping cart and placed it in the back of the truck, shut the gate, and got back in.

"What was that all about?" Bree asked.

"It's a long story," I replied. I put the truck in drive and headed down Holly Drive.

"Ice cream now?" Bree asked.

"One more stop," I said.

I got back on North Kings Highway and headed north. As we drove along Bree talked about work. I tried to pay attention the best I could. When I took a right at Sea Mountain Highway, Bree looked confused. "You're taking me far, far away from where I live," she said in her little girl voice. "Where are we going, mister?"

"It's top secret," I said. I turned onto Ships Wheel Drive, drove to the end of the street, and parked in the turn around.

I pulled the shopping cart out of the back of my truck and wheeled it down a little path that lead from the turnaround to the end of LD Drive. I got in front of the cart and started dragging it into the woods. When I felt I had dragged it to where it needed to be, I returned to the truck.

"I really don't want to know what you're doing, do I?" Bree said in her normal voice.

"Nope," I answered. "Ready for ice cream?"

"Yup. We'll get it to go." I felt her fingers on my thigh again, this time feeling around for the old skin flute, which was just begging to be played.

Oh yeah, I thought. I wanted it to go too. I knew I had a promise coming. I also knew that I had to get home as quick as I could without making it look like I was trying to get home as quick as I could. I didn't know if it was the full moon, or if it was the impending arrival of Hurricane Petrov. All I knew was that the planets had aligned perfectly and Bree was horny. I also knew that any little thing could change that.

Bree waited in the car while I went to the window to order the ice cream. I ordered her a peanut butter sundae with vanilla ice cream, whipped cream, nuts, and a cherry on top. I ordered myself a sundae with vanilla ice cream, strawberry and marshmallow topping, whipped cream, and nuts. I don't like cherries unless they're baked in a pie.

Our sundaes were almost gone when we got to the house.

"You left the garage door open," Bree said, as I pulled into the driveway.

"No I didn't," I said. *Did I?* I wondered. *I don't think I did. Maybe I did.* I wasn't sure. "Wait here." I walked into the garage not knowing for sure if I had left the door open or not, but I did know one thing for sure: this was bound to spoil the mood.

I opened the door to the kitchen and peeked inside. I didn't pull out my weapon, but I pressed my wrist against it to reassure myself that it was there.

The kitchen light was on. I could hear Woofie

barking in the backyard. I knew I didn't leave her outside. I pulled the 9mm, from its holster and quickly made my way through the kitchen, the living room, and out the open sliding glass door onto the patio. Woofie was on the other side of the pool staring at the top of the fence, and barking like a junkyard dog. I ran around the pool, put my foot on the fence rail, and pulled myself up to look over the fence. I could hear someone running through the trees behind my shed.

"Hey!" I shouted. Of course no one answered back.

I dropped back to the concrete. Woofie was still growling. "Good girl," I said. "Who knew miniature Yorkies were such good watchdogs?"

I picked up the dog and on the way back to the truck and I weighed my options. I could tell Bree everything was fine, quickly get her to the bedroom, and then tell her the truth after sex, or tell her the truth now and completely waste this opportunity.

"What's the matter?" Bree asked.

"Someone was in the house," I replied. *So long sexy time*.

Bree put her hand to her mouth. "Oh my God! Who was it?"

I could see the horniness as it escaped her body and evaporated like a ghost in the night breeze. "I have no idea." I handed Woofie to her through the truck window. "Luckily for us, this ferocious guard dog was in there to chase them off."

I pulled out my cell phone and called the station.

"Who are you calling?" Bree asked.

"The fuzz," I replied.

Twenty-Four

I stood on the patio with Lint; we stared at the fence. Bree stood in the doorway holding the dog. "Did you see him go over the fence?" Lint asked.

"No," I replied. "By the time I got out here he was already over and on his way across the neighbor's yard."

"I got a uniform going door to door. Maybe one of your neighbors saw something."

"Probably not."

"Anything missing?"

"Not that we noticed. My revolver was in the nightstand. I checked that first. It's still there."

"Probably who ate the pizza the other day," Bree called out.

"Pizza?" Lint asked.

I rolled my eyes. "She thinks someone ate a few slices of leftover pizza that was in our fridge."

Lint turned to Bree. "When was this?"

Bree looked to me. "Saturday?"

I shrugged. "Yeah, Saturday or Sunday."

"Anything else out of the ordinary?" Lint asked.

"Not really," I answered.

"Not really, or no?"

"Well …"

"Well, what?"

"When I got home from work the other day, the dog was locked in the bedroom. I don't think I would have locked her in there, and I was the last one to leave for work."

"Oh my God!" Bree said. "How many times do you think they've broken in?"

"No sign of forced entry," Lint said.

"Yeah," I agreed.

"You sure the doors were all locked?"

"The front door and the door to the garage both lock automatically. I can't say for sure about the slider. I guess we forget to lock it sometimes. The gate in the fence is always locked, but I guess if someone wanted to climb the fence they could come right in."

"I guess you'll have to start making sure you lock it when you're not home."

"Okay, Jake," Perkins said. Lint and I turned to see him coming through the slider. "They've dusted for prints and they're taking off."

"Okay," I said. "Thanks." I went into the house and Lint followed me. We walked out the garage door and onto the driveway. A white crime scene van sat at the curb; the side and rear doors were open. One of the CSI guys was smoking a cigarette and checking his cell phone. The other guy was loading two tool boxes into the back of the van.

"Thanks, guys," I said, and gave them a little wave.

"No problem, Jake," the smoker said. "We'll get the report to you as quick as we can."

They both climbed into the van and drove off.

I turned to Lint. "I think the bastard kicked my dog," I said.

Lint pointed toward the street. "One of the CSI guys?"

"No," I scolded. "Whoever broke into the house. When I let the dog out of the bedroom the other day, she was limping."

"Prick," said Lint. "Hope he gets the chair."

"Yeah," I agreed.

A squad car pulled up to the end of the driveway; Officers Wang and Clark were inside. Wang was driving; he rolled down his window. "Hey, Jake," he said.

We walked over to the car. "How did it go, guys?" Lint asked.

"Nobody's seen or heard anything," Wang replied. "A guy over behind you—William Dutcher—said he heard his dog barking around that time, but when he went outside he didn't see anything, so he just let his dog back inside."

"Okay, thanks," I said.

"You need us for anything else?" Wang asked.

"No, that's it," Lint replied. "Thanks, guys."

Wang put the car in drive and went up the road with his arm resting out the window.

"Oh, by the way," I said. "We'll be paying the Bowie family a visit tomorrow."

"Why's that?"

"I got an anonymous tip earlier this evening that there's some stolen property on their land."

"There is, is there? And who anonymously tipped you?"

"He wants to remain nameless. I'll fill you in tomorrow morning."

"I can't wait." Lint turned and started toward his brand new Audi, which was parked across the street. "Well, I better get going, we were just heading to dinner when you phoned me."

"Kinda late to be going to dinner, wasn't it?"

Lint turned back. "I've found that folks with a lot of money seem to eat later in the evening."

"Good to know," I said. "Where were you going to dinner tonight?"

"The country club," he answered with a grin.

"The country club," I grumbled.

"Hey, we've invited you guys to the club. You keep turning us down. Bertie wants to introduce you and Bree to some of our friends."

"I can't see myself hanging around the country club with Buffy and Biff."

Lint laughed. "Believe it or not, there's no one named Buffy *or* Biff. You should come some time. You'd like it. Everyone pretends to be really nice. They never say anything mean to your face, they all wait till you walk away. I know they're all wonderful people, because they tell me quite often how wonderful they are."

"They *sound* wonderful."

"They're assholes," Lint said, and climbed in his car.

I walked back through the overhead door and hit the button to close it behind me. I punched the code into the doorknob and went inside. Bree was sitting on the couch with Woofie on her lap. She was watching The Weather Channel again.

I walked to the slider and stood staring out at the backyard. I reached down and slid the door open and then shut the screen.

"What are you doing?" Bree asked.

"Opening the door to get some air in here," I replied. "It's humid as hell, and there's a nice breeze tonight."

"Don't leave it open."

I turned and looked at her. "Bree, I'm not going start leaving every door and window closed because someone broke in the house."

"What if he comes back?"

"He won't come back," I assured her. "He almost got caught this time. He'd have to be pretty stupid to come back." I turned and went back into the kitchen. I pulled open the junk drawer and grabbed a piece of paper that lay on top of everything else we had stuffed in the drawer over the past twelve years. A business card that read MARK GOODIN HOME IMPROVEMENTS was stapled to the top of the page. I walked into the living room reading the paper.

"What's that?" Bree asked.

"The instructions for the door knobs Mark installed," I replied.

"What do you need them for?"

"I don't, but Mark's business card is stapled to the top. I think I'll give him a call in the morning and see if he can recommend someone who installs security systems."

"That would be great," said Bree.

I laid the instructions on the end table so I would see them in the morning and remember to make the call. As I did, something on the floor, just under the edge of my recliner, caught my eye. I glanced back at Bree.

"What?" she asked.

"Nothing," I replied, and sat down.

Bree stared at the television. "Storm's supposed

to hit tonight around midnight," she said. "The eye of the hurricane is forty miles off the coast. We're only supposed to get rain and a little wind; maybe some thunder and lightning."

"Well, that's good." I sat with my fingers interlocked behind my head, watching the television. "So, did you want to go into the bedroom?"

Bree gave me the look of death. "Are you *serious,* Jake?" she asked. "After what happened here tonight?"

"Um, yeah, I was kinda serious."

"It kinda spoiled the mood."

"I'm still in the mood."

"Of course you are." Bree moved the dog off of her lap and stood. "Come on," she said begrudgingly.

"Really?"

She nodded her head toward the sliding glass door. "Yeah, but close that door … and lock it."

"How about if we just do it right here on the couch next to the door?"

"How about if we go out and do it in the front seat of your truck, in the driveway."

"Really! That would be awesome!"

"No, not really. Close the damn door and come to the bedroom."

I quickly put the footrest down and hurried to the door to close it. The couch or the truck would have been fun, but I wasn't turning down the bedroom. I paused for a second until Bree rounded the corner into the hall, then I bent over and grabbed what I had seen under my chair. It was a man's braided necklace. Hanging in the center of the necklace was a small, green, ceramic peace sign. *This ain't mine*, I thought.

"You coming?" Bree shouted from the bedroom.

I shoved the necklace into my front pants pocket, and skipped down the hall like a teenage boy whose girlfriend's parents were out of town.

Twenty-Five

At two thirty in the morning I was awakened by a flash of lightning and the low rumble of thunder. I rolled over and looked at the clock. The lightning flashed again. I waited for the thunder; it came about five seconds later. I could hear the wind and the rain hitting the bedroom window.

I got out of bed and stood in front of the bedroom window and watched the rain. The street was wet but there was no standing water. I was glad of that. I hoped this would be the worst of it. I thought about going into the living room and checking the radar to see how long the storm would last, but I didn't. I stood in front of the window for another minute or two, and then climbed back into bed. I tried to be as careful as I could, not wanting to wake Bree.

As I pulled the blankets up over me and settled in, I heard something. I froze. There it was again, a creaking sound. *What would creak*? I thought. It sounded like the kitchen door.

Woofie let out a little bark. Then I heard what sounded like someone whispering.

The bark woke Bree. "What was that?" she asked.

"The dog barked," I said quietly.

Bree opened her mouth and was about to call the dog. I quickly put one hand over her mouth and with the other I put my index finger to my lips to shush her.

Bree's eyes widened. I pulled my hand away from her mouth. "What is it?" she whispered.

"I thought I heard something," I whispered back.

We could hear Woofie's toenails on the ceramic tile.

I rolled over, opened the nightstand drawer, and grabbed my .45. I searched the floor for my underwear and slipped them on. "Here," I said, handing Bree my cell phone. "I'm going to lock the bedroom door behind me. Call 911, and don't unlock the door until I tell you to." She nodded in agreement. I bent over and reached inside my pants pocket, dropped the pants back on the floor, and went to the door. I turned the lock, and as I stepped into the hall, I looked back and smiled at Bree, she didn't smile back. I quietly closed the door behind me.

I made my way down the hall in my underwear. When I got to the living room, I pressed my back against the wall and peeked in. A man was on his hands and knees with the side of his head resting on the tile. The man's arm was under the couch. Woofie stood next to him, her head cocked to the side.

I stepped into the doorway, reached toward the lamp, and turned it on. The man on the floor jumped to his feet and spun around. Woofie barked. He glanced down at the revolver trained on his chest.

I dangled the necklace from my fingertips. "Looking for this, Mark?" I asked.

Mark Goodin put his hands in the air. "I can explain, Jake," he said.

I pulled back the hammer; it clicked loudly into position. "Can you?" I asked.

A defeated look came over his face. "No."

"I didn't think so. Now turn around, get on your knees, and clasp your fingers behind you head."

"Jake, please—"

"Just do it, Mark."

Mark started to turn, and then somewhere between the lightning's next blinding flash and the loud clap of its thunder, he decided to make a run for it. To where? I can't imagine. Mark took two short steps and tripped over the dog. As the thunder rolled, so did the clumsy thirty-three-year-old door knob installer—head first, right through the sliding glass door. The sound of the breaking glass was much louder than the thunder. He tumbled across the patio and into the pool.

I flipped on the patio light, carefully stepped around the shards of broken glass—so as not to cut my bare feet—and laid my pistol on the wrought-iron table.

"Do you install sliding glass doors, Mark?" I asked. "Or is it just door knobs? Because I think I'm going to need a new slider."

Mark breast-stroked toward the steps. The water around him was turning red. There was a gash over his eye. There was a long slice on his forearm and a big flap of flesh dangled from his arm as he swam. As I helped him out of the pool, I noticed several cuts on his feet and legs.

"Sit down right here," I said.

He sat on the edge of the pool with his feet on the top step. "I'm sorry, Jake," he said.

"You sure are," I replied. "Don't move. I'll run in and grab some towels."

Bree was standing in the doorway. She was holding my cell phone up to her ear. "Watch the glass," I said.

"I will," she said.

"I told you to stay in the bedroom." I grabbed my gun as I walked inside.

"I know, but I heard the glass break and—"

"Tell them to send an ambulance."

"Already did."

I grabbed three or four towels out of the hall closet, and as I rounded the corner into the living room I caught sight of the flashing light bars out of the corner of my eye. I handed the towels to Bree.

"Here, try to stop some of the bleeding," I said. I turned and went to the kitchen door and opened it. I reached into the garage and pressed the button to lift the overhead door. I was still carrying my weapon, so I opened one of the cupboard doors and placed it inside. Then I walked out into the garage with my hands in plain sight.

"Hands in the air!" someone shouted.

"It's Jake!" hollered someone else.

I couldn't see who it was, the lights of the patrol cars were blinding me. There were way more vehicles than were needed, but when the call comes in from a cop's wife, everyone shows up. I shielded my eyes from the headlights.

A large, shadowy figure stepped in front of the headlights and moved toward me. It was Lint. "Get some clothes on," he said. "I pictured you as more of a boxer kinda guy than a tighty-whities man."

I looked down. I was still in my underwear, and they were soaked from very cold pool water. That's when the whistling and catcalls began. It was head cheerleader Daniella Ornoroto all over again. I flipped them the bird and went back inside to get dressed.

Chapter Twenty-Six

The storm had passed. It was warm and sunny. On my way to the station I reflected on the night before: the sex, not the break-in. It was no *Fifty Shades of Grey*, but then again, I had never read or seen *Fifty Shades of Grey*, and damn sure wasn't a kinky billionaire. I could probably turn the guest bedroom into some kind of a weird sex room, but I don't really know what goes inside a sex room. I could Google it I guess, but I wouldn't want that in my search history. As for Mark Goodin, he was in the hospital after his little escapade. There would be time to unravel that mystery later.

I got to the station around nine thirty. Lint was already heavily into paperwork. He looked up when I came through the door.

"Morning, partner," Lint said. "Didn't recognize you with your clothes on."

I glanced around the room. "Morning," I returned quietly.

"Heading over to the Bowies'?" he asked.

I looked up at the clock over the coffee maker as I made my way in that direction. "In a little bit."

"What are we waiting for?"

"A warrant."

"You're getting a warrant?"

"I want this done right. I want that Winchester, and I want it matched to that bullet you pulled out of the siding."

Lint grinned. "I want them to try and stop us like they did the last time we were there."

"Me, too," I said. "But we'll keep that between you and me … partner." The phone on my desk rang. "Stellar," I answered. "Okay, thanks." I hung up the phone and went to Merle's door. "Hey, it's a go."

"Be careful," Merle said.

"Awe," I replied. "That's nice. I will."

"Shut up and get out of here … and close my door."

"Let's roll," I said, as I walked past Lint's desk.

*****

We veered off of Twenty-Seventh Avenue North onto LD Drive. Lint and I were in the lead, riding in the Charger. Behind us were two patrol cars, then Perkins in an unmarked car, with another unit behind him. The North Myrtle Beach Code Enforcement Officer rode alongside Perkins. We moved along at about forty-five miles per hour. An ambulance and an emergency vehicle from the fire department sat at the corner of Little River Neck Road and Twenty-Seventh Avenue … just in case.

I hit the brakes and skidded to a stop in almost the same spot I had parked a day earlier. Pat Murphy pulled up to my right.

Zeke Bowie was hunched over a sawhorse cutting a two-by-six. He dropped the saw when he caught sight of us out of the corner of his eye. He instinctively went for the double-barreled shotgun leaning against the trailer skirting.

I shoved open my door and pulled my weapon as I jumped from the car. "Stop!" I shouted. "North Myrtle Beach Police Department!" I had my weapon trained on a spot between Zeke's shoulder blades. "Don't move!"

Zeke halted and threw his hands in the air.

"On your knees!" Perkins shouted.

The front door of the trailer opened, and Grandma Bowie stepped out onto the deck. She was waving a finger in our direction and shouting.

"Back inside!" Lint hollered. His weapon was already in his hand.

Pat Murphy ran to Zeke and cuffed his hands behind his back.

Grandma slowly backed up toward her door.

"Where's Jesse Bowie?" Lint asked.

Just then the door of the shack opened and Patch stepped onto the porch aiming his 30.06 at no one in particular.

"Put it down!" I hollered.

"Get off my land, you bastards!" Patch shouted back.

The officers next to us took cover behind their car doors with their weapons drawn.

"Put the weapon down," said Lint.

"We have a search warrant," I informed him. "Now put that rifle away."

"Let me see that warrant," Patch ordered.

"Watch him, Lint," I said, and reached inside the car. I grabbed the warrant off the dash board and held it up.

"Bring it here where I kin see it," said Patch.

"Put that rifle down first," I said. The stubborn bastard didn't comply, but rather pointed the weapon at the floor boards. I walked around the car door and made my way toward him. I still had my 9 mm. in my right hand at my side. When I got to Patch I handed him the warrant.

"What are ya searchin' for?" Patch asked as he skimmed over the warrant.

"We have a report of stolen property on the premises, as well as codes violations," I replied.

He glanced over toward the deck. "You sumbitch," he said, and brought the barrel of the gun up.

I lunged toward him, grabbing the barrel with my left hand and smashing the grip of my 9mm against the side of his head. Patch's head snapped to the side and he hit the floor on his hip and shoulder, unconscious.

"Pa!" I heard someone yell behind me. Then I heard a shot. The bullet hit the wooden support post beside me. I spun around to see Jesse Bowie running across his grandmother's deck with the Winchester 33 in his hands.

Lint fired, hitting Jesse in the shoulder, spinning him around. He hit the deck on his side and tumbled down the steps.

Ronnie Pierce ran from behind the passenger side door toward Jessie. He dropped and pressed one knee into the kid's back. "Hold still," Ronnie said, cuffing him.

Grandma reached down and picked up the Winchester. "You shot my grandson!" she screeched. She pointed the rifle at Ronnie.

Ronnie jumped up and rolled behind the trailer.

Grandma turned and saw that every weapon was pointing at her. She froze.

"Lay it on the deck," Lint said calmly.

Grandma did as she was told.

I looked down; Patch was coming to. I cuffed his hands in front of him. "Just sit right there," I said. "Perkins, get that ambulance down here."

Ronnie came out from behind the trailer. "Come here," I said. I pointed toward the woods. "Check the property for anything that might be stolen."

Ronnie gave a quizzical look. "What exactly am I looking for?" he asked.

I shrugged. "Anything. Maybe something stolen from a store."

"What kinda store?"

"Shit, Pierce!" I whispered. "Like a grocery store, maybe. Just go look around."

Ronnie turned and walked into the woods.

Lint walked over and handed me the .33. "Looks like this could be the weapon used in the murder."

Patch's eyes widened. "Murder! What murder?"

I looked down at Patch. Blood ran from the side of his head down his cheek and dripped off his chin. "Mittens," I said.

Patch looked confused. "Who the hell is Mittens?"

"She was one of your neighbors, ya prick," answered Lint. "And your boy shot her."

I looked toward Perkins' car. "Where the hell is that codes enforcer guy?" I asked.

Lint shrugged. "I have no idea."

I walked around to the passenger side of the car

and looked in. The pencil-pushing coward was curled up on the floor. "It's all clear," I said.

"Um, yeah," he replied. "I dropped my pen down here." He climbed out of the car. "What's the suspected codes violation?" he asked.

I pointed at the deck Zeke was building. "I don't think they got a permit for that."

The officer carried his clipboard toward the deck. He reached into a bag of nails and held one up to me. "These gotta be galvanized," he said.

"Yeah, whatever," I replied. "Write him up."

Ronnie Pierce came dragging the shopping cart out of the woods. "Found a stolen shopping cart!" he shouted.

"You sumbitches!" Patch hollered. "I'll get you for this!"

"Is he threatening police officers?" Lint asked.

"I think he is," I replied.

"Better add that to the list."

My cell phone rang. I reached into my pocket and pulled it out. "Stellar," I said.

"Jake, it's Merle. Just got a call from Ted Gaffney's lawyer. Lucy Gaffney is recanting her statement. She's saying she wasn't with the Blasting boy the night of the murder."

"You're kidding," I replied in disbelief.

"She says she made up the story to protect him."

Chapter Twenty-Seven

Lucy Gaffney had lied in her statement, which meant she had to come back in for questioning. She tried to get out of it, but I explained to her that she didn't have a choice at this point. So, later that afternoon, Ted Gaffney, Lucy, and her lawyer, Blaine Hestor, returned to interrogation room number one.

"So why did you lie?" I asked.

Lucy glanced over at her lawyer. He nodded his head and she looked back at me. "Because I didn't want him to get into any trouble."

"Terry Blasting?"

She shot me a well, duh look. Once a snotty bitch, always a snotty bitch.

"Answer him, Lucy," Hestor said firmly.

"Yes."

"Trouble for what?" I asked.

"Killing Mrs. Truman."

"You think Terry killed Mrs. Truman?"

"Maybe."

"Maybe? Did he tell you he killed her?"

"No."

"Then what makes you think he did?"

"He left my house earlier than I said."

"What time did he leave?"

"Around eight o'clock."

"Did you speak to him again that night?"

"No."

"When was the next time you spoke with him?"

"The next day … after he found Mrs. Truman."

"What did he say to you?"

"He asked me to tell the police that he had stayed at my house until eleven or after."

"Who asked Valerie Marrero to lie?" I asked.

Lucy raised her cavewoman eyebrows questioningly to her lawyer; he nodded. "I did," she replied.

I looked at Ted Gaffney. "Did you know she lied?" I asked.

"I just found out this morning," Gaffney replied. "As soon as she told me, I informed Blaine, and he called you."

My eyes went back to Lucy. "When I question Valerie will she say the same thing?"

Lucy shrugged. "I don't know."

"Why wouldn't she?"

"I don't know. Maybe she doesn't want to get into trouble, or maybe she doesn't want to get Terry into trouble."

"I don't think it's possible for Terry to get into any more trouble," I reminded her.

"I know, but maybe she wouldn't want to hurt his parents, or maybe she wouldn't want to say bad things about him now that he's dead. She's known him and his family for a long time. She was really close with them. Maybe she was even in on it."

Hestor grabbed her arm and gently squeezed, telling her to stop talking.

I raised my brow. That was something I hadn't expected her to say. I doubt Hestor saw that coming either. "In on it?" I asked.

"I don't know, maybe—"

Hestor spoke up, interrupting his client. "What Lucy means is, she has no idea whether Miss Marrero will or will not recant her statement, and can only guess why she wouldn't."

"Lucy, did Valerie leave with Terry?" I asked.

"No," said Lucy. "She spent the night."

"Did Valerie say or do anything that lead you to believe she was involved in the death of Wanda Truman?"

"No."

"You said Valerie would continue to lie because she wouldn't want to get into trouble. Why would she get into trouble?"

Lucy sat silent for a moment, and then she said, "Because she didn't really spend the night at my house. She left around seven thirty."

"Where did she go?"

"I don't know."

Hestor scooted his chair back. "If that's all, Detective …"

I didn't answer. I knew I could hold Lucy on her false statement, but it would be a waste of time. Hestor would have her out within the hour.

Lucy and her father got up and they all three left the room.

I got up as well and went into the squad room. I watched as the trio exited the building through the squad room door into the parking lot, then I turned and walked into the lounge. Valerie Marrero and her father sat on the leather sofa, and Lint sat in one of the two chairs across from them. Valerie was drinking a can of Diet Coke. Lint's legs were crossed with the case file in his lap. He flipped through papers and photographs.

"Sorry to keep you waiting," I said.

"That's okay," Valerie said.

"Why are we here?" Cecil Marrero demanded.

I sat in the chair next to Lint. "Valerie, tell me

again, when did Terry Blasting leave the Gaffneys' house the night of the murder?"

She looked at her father and then back at me. "It was after eleven thirty … close to midnight, I think."

"You think?"

"I'm sure it was after eleven-thirty."

"What time did you leave?" I asked.

"I stayed the night, and then went home early the next morning."

"We were going out of town Saturday morning," Cecil added. "I told her if she was spending the night she had to be home by seven in the morning."

"Lucy changed her story," I said.

"What do you mean, 'changed it'?" Valerie asked.

"She's saying that Terry Blasting left her house around eight o'clock that night."

"That's not true," Valerie shot back.

"She says the two of you made up the story to protect Terry."

"She's lying."

"She also says you didn't sleep at her house that night. She says you left around seven-thirty."

Cecil's eyes focused on his little girl. "Valerie, is this true?" he asked.

"Yes, Daddy." Valerie put her head down.

"Where were you?" Cecil asked.

"Eddie's."

Cecil put his hand on her back. He was a lot more understanding than I thought I would be.

"Who's Eddie?" Lint asked.

"He's my boyfriend," Valerie answered.

Lint pulled a blank sheet of paper out of the file folder and laid it on the coffee table in front of her. He took a pen out of his shirt pocket and placed it next to the paper. "Write down his name and phone number … please."

Valerie leaned over the table and started writing. A tear fell and hit the paper.

"Why did you lie about Terry being there until midnight?" I asked.

"I didn't want my dad to find out," she replied. "And I didn't want Terry to get in any trouble. He wouldn't have done anything like that. I know he wouldn't."

When Valerie finished writing, Cecil asked if there were any more questions. I told him no, but that we may have more questions later.

Lint picked up the paper and slipped it back into the folder.

Cecil hugged his daughter and the two of them left, closing the door behind them.

"What now?" Lint asked.

"Call that Eddie kid and make sure Valerie was really there," I said.

"Then what?"

"Then I'm going home. I'm tired."

"Oh yeah," Lint recalled. "You didn't get much sleep last night running around in your underwear." He chuckled a little.

"Shut up."

Lint put up his hands in defeat. "I know, I know, the pool water was cold. Don't worry, everyone knows about shrinkage."

I had no response, but it did help me decide to go home then, instead of waiting until after Lint made his phone call.

Chapter Twenty-Eight

Instead of going home, I decided to take a ride by the hospital. I parked, went inside, and rode the elevator up to the second floor. I stopped at the nurses station and asked what room Mark Goodin was in.

A uniformed police officer sat in a chair in front of Mark's door; he stood when he saw me round the corner.

"How's it going, Detective?" the young officer asked.

"Good," I said, and went in.

Mark lay in his bed with his arms at his side. He had a bandage over his eye, and his left arm was bandaged from his wrist to his armpit. The television was turned on, but the volume was almost all the way down. He looked over when he saw me come in.

"How's it going, Mark?" I asked.

He lifted his right arm to show me he was handcuffed to the bed rail. "Wonderful," he replied.

"You didn't lose the arm, I see."

"Seventy-something stitches."

I looked over and stared at the television for a few seconds. An infomercial for one of those stupid gadgets I couldn't possibly live without was on. I don't know if I was waiting for an apology, or what, but one didn't come.

"Why, Mark?" I asked, not taking my eyes from the TV. I anticipated the "But wait, there's more!" pitch line. Bingo, there it was.

"My lawyer said not to speak to the cops unless he's here."

"Really, Mark? That's how you want this to go?" I looked over at him. There was a lot of remorse on his face—more than I'm used to seeing on the average perp. "If you don't talk to me, I can't help you."

He didn't say anything.

"Who's your attorney?" I asked.

"Some guy named Bouchard," Mark said. "The court appointed him. He's supposed to be here tomorrow morning."

"Mark, I looked you up before I ever hired you. You have no priors. You've never been in any trouble at all. I couldn't even find where you had ever had a parking ticket. Why would you break into my house?"

Mark stared at the television. "I'm broke, Jake."

"Broke? How broke?"

"I don't have any money. The last job I did was your door knobs. Seventy-five bucks don't go very far."

"Why didn't you say something?"

"What was I supposed to say? 'Hey, Jake, we don't really know each other that well, but I just got kicked out of my apartment. Can I borrow some money?'"

"You lost your apartment? Where have you been staying?"

"In my truck, in the Walmart parking lot."

"Jesus, Mark. How did this happen?"

"I'm just not good with money. I had a dry spell with hardly any work. I had no savings. This business isn't what it was just fifteen years ago. You need to be licensed for this, licensed for that, permits for every goddamn thing you do. They nickel and dime you so bad you have to raise your prices so high that most people can't afford to hire you."

"How many times have you broken into our house?"

"Five or six," he replied ashamedly.

"Five or six! We didn't notice anything missing."

"I didn't take anything. I looked around for cash a couple times, but you never had any laying around. Mostly I just watched TV and grabbed something to eat."

"Pizza?"

"Yeah, I finished that pizza. Sorry about that. I was hungry. Tell Bree that chili was awesome too. She should probably put some meat in it though."

"That's what I said. Did you kick my dog, Mark?"

"Kick your dog? Why would I kick your dog? I love that little dog." Mark looked back at the television. "That dog was good company whenever I was there."

"She was limping one day when I got home, and she was locked in the bedroom."

"I stepped on her toe on accident, and put her on the bed before I left. I must have shut the door without realizing it."

"Just checking."

"I'm really sorry, Jake."

"I know you are, Mark. Listen, we're going to get you out of here. I'll call your lawyer tonight." I paused and thought for a second. "Was my house the only house?"

Mark shook his head. "No. There was a house over on Surf Street, the Mulligans."

"Someone you work for?"

"Yeah. I went in and took five hundred bucks."

"I'll check and see if they reported it."

"They didn't. They live in Ohio and don't get into town until the middle of November. They're snowbirds and happened to mention that to me when I was doing an installation there. I was hoping I could put the money back before they arrive."

"Okay, Mark, don't mention that to anyone, not even your lawyer. You got it?"

"Yes."

"I'll stop back by tomorrow afternoon."

"Thanks, Jake."

"Don't make me regret this." I turned and left.

Chapter Twenty-Nine

When I got home Luca Trentinni was standing in my living room facing the patio door, with his hands on his hips. He was marveling at the great job he had done of duct taping large pieces of cardboard to the window frames. He had also swept up all the broken glass. He spun around when he heard me enter. It was probably his ninja hearing that allowed him to detect me as I crossed the tile.

"Jake!" he said, a little too enthusiastically. He waved his arm toward the door. "What do you think?"

"I didn't know you were such a handy guy," I replied. "Thanks, Luca."

"Don't mention it."

I looked around. "Where are the ladies?"

"They went to pick up Chinese food." Luca was sliding the door open and closed to make sure nothing got hung up on the cardboard or duct tape. He stepped back and nodded approvingly.

"Did you get yourself something to drink?" I asked. "There's a few beers in the fridge, I think."

"I grabbed a water."

"I'm going to jump in the shower." I turned and went down the hall.

"I'll be here."

"I know you will," I mumbled.

"What's that?"

"Nothing."

While I showered I spent the entire time wondering if Luca was looking around our house to see just how poor we were compared to him and Aida. Bree and I weren't really poor by any means, but I wondered if people like Luca and Aida—and now even Avis and Birtie—thought we were. Luca's swimming pool was twice the size of mine. Luca's house was twice the size of mine. Luca's paycheck was at least seven times what mine was. I guess these things wouldn't bother me so much if Luca acted like a regular guy, but he never did. He was just not my kind of person, not the kind of guy I would normally hang around with; I mean, if I decided to make friends and start hanging around with someone. *Holy shit*, I thought. *I don't have any friends. What the hell is wrong with me? Dammit! Did I already wash my hair? I can't remember. Friggin Luca!*

I wrapped a towel around me and walked from the bathroom to the bedroom to get dressed. I sure as hell wouldn't make the trip naked. Luca probably had a dick twice the size as mine. *I need a beer. Why did Bree invite them over for dinner?* I hoped it wasn't because he volunteered to fix the door. I could have fixed that myself. I'm not a handyman, but it was cardboard and duct tape for Chrissakes.

Luca was on the patio drinking a bottle of beer when I walked outside with my glass of ginger ale. Over twelve years without a drink, but I still liked to drink my ginger ale in a rocks glass over ice to fool my brain into thinking I was having a good time. Sometimes I would even drop in a lime or lemon wedge.

Luca sat at the wrought-iron table, pen in hand, finishing my crossword puzzle. It wasn't the puzzle from this morning's newspaper, it was one from a week ago. I had been working on it slowly in my spare time. I was more than half finished.

I sat in the chair across from him and set my glass on the table.

Luca took a sip from his bottle. "Good beer," he said, as he read the label. "Goose Island IPA. Where did this come from?"

"I don't know," I replied. "Someone left it here after the last cookout."

"It's good." He took another swig.

"Glad you like it," I said. Luca and I didn't have much to talk about. It was always the same. After a few minutes of silence he would ask me about work. I would tell him what I was working on in as few words as possible. He would nod his head as though he was interested. After a few more moments of listening to the pool pump run I would ask him about his work and he would say a bunch of shit that I wouldn't listen to, because then I would be thinking about my own work. I would be wondering why Lucy Gaffney changed her story. I would be wondering why Wanda Truman wanted her husband dead, but most of all I would be wondering who hit Wanda in the head with a gray metal pipe and then threw her into her own pool. I would be wondering if ballistics came back on the Bowie rifle. I wondered how Mark Goodin was doing, handcuffed to his hospital bed, and what I was going to say to his attorney. I didn't want that kid going to jail. He was a good kid.

The pool pump hummed.

"So," Luca asked. "How's work going?"

"Good," I answered.

"What are you working on at the moment?"

"A lady was murdered and thrown in her pool to make it look like an accident."

"I read about that."

"Uh-huh."

Luca filled in the last three squares of my puzzle and dropped the pen like it was a microphone at the end of a heated rap battle. "Done," he said, as though he was being timed.

I wondered if I stabbed him with the pen and threw him in my pool if it would look like an accident. *Where are Bree and Aida?* I wondered. I heard the kitchen door slam shut. *Thank God!*

I turned to look through the sliding glass door, but then remembered it was solid cardboard.

Bree stepped through the door onto the patio. "We're back," she announced. "The door looks great, Luca. Thank you so much."

It's just cardboard and duct tape, I thought.

"No problem," Luca replied. "I figured Jake would be tired after work and not feel like doing home repairs." He grinned and looked my way. "Am I right, pal?"

"You're right," I agreed.

Aida walked through the door holding a beer. "Hey, Jake," she said.

"Aida," I returned.

"Did you find someone to replace the door?" Bree asked.

"Yes," I said.

"Who?"

"We'll talk about it later."

"Is it a secret?"

"Who did you get, Jake?" Luca asked. "You're regular contractor is in jail." He chuckled. "Let me give you the name of my guy."

"I don't need the name of anyone's guy," I said. "And he's not in jail, he's in the hospital."

Luca laughed. "Probably shackled to the bed."

Stabbing him with the pen was looking better and better. I wonder if it's even possible to stab a bodybuilding ninja with a pen. It would probably bounce off his muscles—that is, if you were fast enough to get past those ninja reflexes. I think I saw someone try to stab Jason Bourne with a pen once, and it didn't end well for that guy.

"Who did you get to replace it?" Bree asked again.

"Mark is going to replace it," I admitted.

"Mark. Mark Goodin?"

"Yes, Mark Goodin."

Luca and Aida looked at each other with that oh-no-there's-about-to-be-a-fight look. There wasn't about to be a fight—a small argument maybe, but not a fight.

"He's a criminal," Bree said angrily.

"He's not a criminal." I was wishing someone was getting murdered somewhere in the city so I would be rescued by a phone call.

"Breaking into someone's home makes you a criminal," Bree informed me.

"Oh," I said. "That's what makes someone a criminal? I've only been in law enforcement for twenty years. I've been wondering what makes a criminal."

"Oh, that's great," Bree said.

"Are you sure it's a good idea?" Luca asked.

"I'm sure Jake knows what he's doing," Aida threw in. At least someone was on my side.

"Mark is putting in the new door," I said. "That's it. End of story."

Bree had a scary talent. When she was really pissed she could throw her voice through her gritted teeth like a ventriloquist. "And I have no say about this?" Bree asked.

"No."

I slept on the couch that night.

Chapter Thirty

Mark Goodin was released from the hospital on Saturday morning and taken directly to the J. Reuben Long Detention Center to await his arraignment—which would be later that afternoon. I had already spoken with Mark's attorney. I explained to Edgar Bouchard that I would not be pressing charges, but that that might not be enough to get the district attorney to drop the case. I told him I would try and speak with the DA before the hearing.

I showed up at the courthouse a little before two. Mark was glad to see me; so was Bouchard. I recognized Bouchard as soon as I saw him. I had dealt with him once in the past. At the station we referred to him as The Pig-Man, because of his pug nose and saggy jowls. The first time I laid eyes on him, I was sure he had escaped from Dr. Moreau's island.

Bouchard was grinning as I walked down the

hallway toward them. He stuck out his hand. "Detective Jake Stellar," he said. "It's a marvelous thing you're doing for this boy." He spoke in a deep Southern accent, the kind reserved only for Charleston's elite. Bouchard was a lawyer Mark would never be able to afford, but luckily for Mark, even Bouchard had to put in some pro bono time for the dregs of humanity.

I shook Bouchard's hand. "We've met before," I informed him.

"I recall," said Bouchard. "When you falsely accused that poor Oriental boy of murder." He said murder slowly and ominously as though thunder would clap after he said it.

I ignored the jab. "Are they on schedule?" I asked.

"We're up next," said Mark. "I'm nervous."

"You should be," I said.

Bouchard slapped Mark on the back. "You have nothing to worry about, boy. You simply returned to a previous place of employment to retrieve a piece of personal property. You didn't know the Stellars were at home, so, knowing the entrance code, you simply entered as you had done in the past." He smiled in pride at his concocted story. I think I may have even heard a faint squeal of excitement.

"That's not how the story's going to go," I informed Bouchard.

"Of course it is," Bouchard argued.

I shook my head. "No, we're all going to tell the truth, and hope for the best."

"I think we better stick with my story," said Bouchard.

"Not if you want me in there standing next to you," I said. "Mark, you decide. How do you want this to go?"

Mark didn't hesitate. "I think I should tell the truth."

"I think you're making a big mistake, boy," Bouchard said.

"Not as big as the one's I've already made. We'll stick with the truth.

The large oak doors leading to the courtroom opened and a bailiff stuck his head through the opening. "Mark Goodin," he said.

We all looked at each other.

"Here goes nothin'," Mark said.

*****

Mark's hearing went better than expected. The judge released him without bail. In order for that to happen, I had to tell the judge that he would be staying at my house while he was working there—something I hadn't discussed with Bree ahead of time.

Bouchard put his arm around Mark as we walked back through the oak doors. "Didn't I say you had nothing to worry about, boy," he said.

"Yeah," Mark replied. "Thanks, Mr. Bouchard."

Bouchard shook my hand as he grinned proudly. "I'll see you gentlemen next month at the trial," he said, "unless I can get these charges dropped before then." He leaned closer to Mark. "Might be a good idea to have your own place by then, just in case. It'll look good to the judge."

"I will, Mr. Bouchard," said Mark.

Bouchard tipped his fedora, turned, and waddled down the corridor.

"Thanks, Jake," Mark said, when Bouchard was out of ear-shot.

"Don't worry about it, kid," I said. "Now let's go get your truck and the rest of your shit and get it to my house." We headed down the hall toward the exit.

"This is awful nice of you and Mrs. Stellar to let me stay with you guys," Mark said.

"Well, she doesn't exactly know about it yet," I admitted. "So you're going to wait in the driveway until I tell her."

Mark held the door for me and I walked outside first. "That's fine. I don't think I would want to be in there when you tell her anyway."

Chapter Thirty-One

Mark put his tools in the garage and what few things he had packed in boxes in the spare bedroom where he was going to be sleep. Talking Bree into letting him stay for a few weeks was easier than I thought it was going to be. I think when she looked out the kitchen window and saw him sitting all alone and friendless in his truck in the driveway she felt bad for him.

I knew having him stay with us was going to be just as good for me as it was for Mark. Now I had someone to mow the lawn, clean the pool, and paint over the black spot on the siding. He also said he knew how to install security cameras and motion sensors. He seemed to know how to do a little bit of everything, a real jack-of-all-trades. I wondered if I should show him the case file for the Truman murder—maybe he knew how to solve crimes as well.

Mark began replacing the sliding glass door the first thing Sunday morning. He joked that he couldn't believe I was replacing it, because Luca's cardboard installation job looked so nice. I had to pay for the door and the rest of the materials of course, because Mark had no money.

Sunday evening, the two of us drove over to the Mulligan's place on Surf Street and Mark put back the five hundred dollars he had stolen; that five hundred dollars also came from me. All told, I was out approximately seventeen hundred dollars. Mark assured me that he would repay me as quickly as he could. I told him he could pay back the five hundred, but as far as the rest of it, he would be working that off.

Monday morning, Bree and I had to work, Mark started right in on painting the living room.

Bree and I stood in the driveway next to my truck. "Are you sure it's okay to leave him here alone?" Bree asked.

"Of course," I said. "Why wouldn't it be?"

"Because he's a criminal."

"He's not a criminal."

"Are we going to have this conversation again?"

"The kid made a mistake, and now he's paying for it. Would you rather he went to jail?"

"I guess not."

"Everyone deserves a second chance."

Bree's eyes almost bugged out of her head. "Everyone deserves a second chance?" she repeated.

"Did you hit your head at work? This is not like you. You hate everyone."

"I don't hate everyone," I argued.

"Name someone you like."

I thought for a second. "Wesley Crusher," I said.

"Who the hell is Wesley Crusher?"

"He was that kid on *Star Trek: The Next Generation*," I explained. "He was smart, polite, and always willing to help out."

Bree stared at me blankly. "That's a television show, Jake."

"You didn't say it had to be a real person."

Bree leaned in for a kiss. "I gotta go. I don't have time for your foolishness." She kissed me on the lips and said, "I love you."

"I love you too," I replied.

*****

As soon as I walked through the door Lint said, "Hey. That ballistics report from the Bowie escapade is on your desk."

"Is it a match?" I asked.

"Didn't look," List responded.

I stowed my weapon in my top desk drawer, and went to the coffee machine. "Where the hell is the coffee machine?" I asked.

Lint looked up from his desk. "Oh, Merle broke it."

"How?"

"He was going to clean the pot and he dropped it."

"Clean the pot? Why would he clean the pot?"

"He said it was filthy."

"Yeah it was filthy. Coffee pots are supposed to be filthy. Once you wash the pot, the coffee tastes like shit."

"I guess no one explained coffee pot etiquette to him."

"I guess not. What am I supposed to drink?"

"There's water in the fridge, in the break room."

"Forget it," I said, and returned to my desk. I opened the folder and began reading the ballistics report. The findings were inconclusive. The bullet Lint had pulled from the Moons' siding was too deformed to get a match. According to Conrad Moon, there were two shots fired, which meant there was another bullet somewhere. I wondered if it was inside Mittens.

"What's it say?" Lint asked.

"Inconclusive," I replied. "We need that other bullet."

"You want me to go and dig it out of Mittens?"

"No." I picked up my desk phone. "You got the Moons' phone number right there?" I asked.

Lint shuffled through some folders on his desk and then flipped one open. He read the number to me.

"Good morning," I began. "Is this Carlton Moon?"

"Yup it is," Carlton answered.

"Carlton, this is Detective Jake Stellar. We spoke the other day at your home."

"Yes, Detective. How can hep ya? I see you 'rested those Bowie boys the other day. Been purdy quiet round here since then. Maybe we'll get some jestice fer our little Mittens."

"Well, that's what I'm calling about. Seems the bullet we took out of your siding wasn't in good enough shape to get a match with Bowie's rifle."

"So then you cain't charge him with Mitten's killin', can ya?"

"Only if we get the other bullet."

"But that's still in—"

"I know."

"So nothin's gonna hap'in to him?"

"Not exactly," I explained. "Jesse Bowie was arrested for resisting arrest, discharging a weapon within city limits, possession of stolen property, possession of a controlled substance, first-degree attempted murder, criminal use of a firearm, and a buttload of other charges, so even without the cruelty to animals charge, he's going away for long time."

"Couldn't happen to a nicer boy," said Carlton. "We'll leave that other bullet right where it is, and just tell Maw that boy's goin' away for killin' Mittens. She won't know none the better."

"Your secret is safe with me, Carlton."

"Thanks, Jake. That was some real backwoods shit you pulled there."

I laughed. "We always get them in the end, Carlton. We always get them in the end. You have a nice day, sir."

"I will now, you do the same," said Carlton, and he hung up.

When I hung up the phone I looked over at Lint, he was staring at me with a grin.

"What?" I asked.

"Nothing," he replied.

"If you got something to say, say it."

"You're turning into a real softy."

"Bullshit."

"Bullshit? You did all that for a dead cat."

"I did it because Jesse Bowie is a piece of shit and North Myrtle Beach is a better place without him in it."

Lint was still smiling. He coughed into his hand and said "softy" at the same time.

"Whatever," I replied. I was getting pretty good at my comebacks as well.

Lint closed the file he was working on. "What's next?" he asked.

"Arrest whoever murdered Wanda Truman."

"And when do you want to do that?"

"As soon as we figure out who killed her."

"And *how* do you want to do that?"

"With deductive reasoning," I replied. "Just like Sherlock Holmes used to do."

"Do you have his number?" Lint joked.

"I wish."

"John Truman had means and motive, but no opportunity," Lint threw out.

"And Terry Blasting had means and opportunity, but no motive," I added. "Who had motive?"

"The lawnmower."

I chuckled. "To kill John, maybe, but not Wanda."

"The lawnmower's husband might have been angry enough."

"Let's put that on the back burner. Who else was angry enough?"

"The only person who was angry enough to want someone dead was Wanda Truman."

"Angry enough, or greedy enough. We'll never know for sure."

"Maybe Lucy Gaffney really knew what was going on between Wanda and Terry Blasting. Maybe she knew Wanda had offered him sex after he murdered John Truman. Maybe she was in love with Terry and killed Wanda out of jealousy."

"A bunch of maybes there."

Lint searched his notes. "The pastor at the church hinted that there may have been more to Lucy and Terry's relationship than just being friends."

"Lucy argued about that though."

"She admitted to lying. Maybe she lied about that as well."

"Maybe."

"Pastor Parks also said she had some anger issues. He said she was pretty angry when she started the bereavement group."

"But she was angry at her father. What would Wanda's death have to do with being angry with her father?"

"Nothing I can think of."

I locked my fingers behind my head and leaned back in my chair. "A girl with a dead mother, a boy with a dead sister, they become unlikely friends, and then a woman ends up dead. It's got to be connected."

Lint was still reading through his notes. "Terry Blasting's sister died at the hospital where Wanda worked. There's a connection."

"Wanda worked in the allergy, asthma, and sinus clinic. She probably didn't see many cancer patients."

"Her boss, Carol Tyne—she was angry enough to kill Wanda."

"She had an alibi, so did her husband, and so did the other two guys and their wives."

"Maybe there's a guy we don't know about."

I looked up at the clock. "Could be."

"The only others we've questioned are the Marreros—all three of them have alibis—and Ted Gaffney, he also has an alibi."

"Does he?" I asked.

"Yes. Lucy said he went—"

"Yeah, Lucy said. Lucy and Ted are pretty much each other's alibi."

"Ted could be lying to protect his daughter."

"Or her, him."

"Why would Ted Gaffney want Wanda dead? Wanda didn't work in the emergency room, and even if she had, they didn't even make it to the hospital; Ted's wife died in the car on the way."

I took out my cell phone and called Bree; I got her voicemail. "Hey, can you give me a call when you get this message? Love ya." I hung up.

"Having lunch with Bree again?" Lint asked.

"No. Just have a couple questions for her about the night Ted brought in his wife." I looked up at the clock again. "I think I'm going home for lunch and check on Mark."

"Mark? Mark who?"

"Mark Goodin. I've got him painting the living room today."

"The Mark Goodin who broke into your house and crashed through your sliding glass door?"

"One and the same." I got up, retrieved my weapon, and headed toward the door.

"Why would you have him working for you?"

"Because."

As I let the door shut behind me I heard Lint shout: "Softy!"

Chapter Thirty-Two

Mark had the living room all done when I got home—walls, trim, *and* ceiling. It would have taken me three days. He'd done a neat professional job; there wasn't a single line in the paint left by the roller. I always leave those damn lines. The lawn was mowed, and he even swept the grass clippings off the sidewalk and driveway.

I slid the new door open and walked out onto the patio. Mark was vacuuming the pool. Is there anything this kid couldn't do? I wondered if I could hire him to take my place alongside Bree at the mall.

An open bottle of Goose Island Ale was on the patio table.

"Living room looks great," I said.

"Probably need a second coat," Mark replied.

"Really? Looks pretty good to me."

"We can leave it then."

"No, you do whatever you think."

"I grabbed a beer out of the fridge," Mark said, motioning toward the table. "I hope you don't mind."

"Help yourself," I responded.

"You home for the day?"

"No. Just grabbing lunch."

"I made tuna salad and had a sandwich earlier. I put the rest in a Tupperware container in the fridge. Should be enough for a couple more sandwiches."

I turned and went back inside. The tuna salad was right where Mark said it was, and there was even a lid on the Tupperware container.

I removed my pistol and placed it in the cupboard over the microwave, then threw four pieces of toast in the toaster, and grabbed the butter out of the fridge. When the toast popped up, I buttered all four slices and split the remainder of the tuna between the two sandwiches. It really was tuna salad, not just tuna. A lot of people open a can of tuna, mix in a little mayo, and call it tuna salad. Mark actually made tuna salad. There were bits of onion, celery, pickle, and even a little green pepper in there.

Mark entered the kitchen just as I tossed the empty container into the sink. "You do the dishes?" I asked.

"Yeah," Mark replied. "There were only a few."

"I can't believe you found the right lid for the Tupperware. Bree and I—okay, mainly me — are bad about putting them just any old where in the cupboard."

"I kinda noticed that," Mark grinned. "I stacked all the containers according to size, and put the lids on their sides next to them. And I hope you don't mind, but I threw out all of the Cool-Whip and I Can't Believe It's Not Butter containers."

"No, that's fine," I said, stepping over to the cupboard and opening the door for inspection. "Wow." The cupboard looked just like what I would imagine Gordon Ramsey's cupboard would look like. "Bree's going to love that."

I placed my sandwiches on a plate and went into the living room to enjoy them with a little television. I sat down in the recliner, put up my feet, and grabbed the remote. "Dammit!"

"What's the matter?" Mark called out.

"Forgot to get something to drink," I replied.

"Stay right there. I'll get it. What do you want, a ginger ale?"

"That would be great." Holy shit, it was just like having my own butler.

Mark brought me my drink in a flash; it was in a rocks glass with a lime wedge. "How's that sandwich?" he asked.

"Fantastic," I said, and turned on the TV; *The Love Boat* was on. Can it get any better than this? I thought as I watched Isaac the bartender mix up a margarita for a woman with a Pat Benatar haircut and way too much blue eye shadow. Mark went back outside to finish cleaning the pool.

Just about the time I was done with my lunch, my cell phone rang; it was Bree. "Hello?" I said.

"You called?" she asked.

"Yes, I did."

"What's up?"

"Guess what I'm doing?"

"I can't imagine."

"I'm sitting in my recliner in my freshly painted living room watching TV and eating the tuna salad that Mark prepared for lunch. I'm also drinking a glass of ginger ale he made me … with a lime wedge."

"Well, isn't that—"

"Wait, I'm not finished. He's out there right now cleaning the pool."

"Seems your man Friday is going to save you from doing a lot of work."

"I think it's going to work out just as well for you. He rearranged the Tupperware cupboard."

"What was he doing in the cupboards?"

"Looking for a container for my tuna salad … and it's really tuna *salad,* not just tuna with mayo."

"That's great, Jake."

"What do you think I should have him do next?"

"I don't know, but is this why you called me at work?"

"Oh … no. I was calling to ask how easy you

thought it would be to find out who was working in the emergency room on certain night a year ago September."

"Not hard at all," Bree replied. "I can't look it up from where I am, but someone in HR could look it up for you."

"I wonder how long the hospital keeps old security footage."

"That I wouldn't know."

"One more thing. How much of what goes on does a doctor write in his notes?"

"I don't know what you mean."

"Well, for example, would a doctor or nurse write down what a patient or a patient's spouse says in the ER during treatment?"

"That all depends on the doctor. Maybe if it was something relevant to the diagnosis or something he or she felt they might be asked about later."

"Okay, thanks. Maybe I'll stop over this afternoon and see if someone can look those things up for me."

"I get out at three, why don't you come tomorrow morning when I'm here. That way I can go down to HR with you."

"Sounds good," I agreed. "Well, I better get back to work. Love ya."

"Love you too."

"Oh, and he did the dishes too."

"That's great, Jake. Bye."

"Bye." I got up and put my plate in the sink and then went to the back door. "Hey, I'm heading back to work."

Mark gave me the thumbs up. "You need me to do anything after I finish the pool?" he asked.

"Not that I can think of," I replied.

"Okey dokey." He gave me the thumbs up again. "What time do you usually get home from work?"

"A little after five, usually."

"And Bree?"

"A little after four."

"See ya later then."

I went to the cupboard, grabbed my gun, shoved it into its holster, and headed for my truck.

Chapter Thirty Three

I met Bree in the ER at ten o'clock Tuesday morning. First she took me down to human resources to meet with a woman by the name of Tanya Wood. Tanya was more than happy to help me, and printed out a list of doctors and nurses who were working in the emergency room the evening Ted Gaffney brought in his wife. I was in luck: for several years it had been hospital policy for all security camera footage to be loaded up routinely to a cloud-based storage service. Tanya copied onto a thumb drive security footage from three different cameras that started a half hour before Gaffney arrived, to a half hour after he left. According to records, it was Dr. Bruce Ryder who worked on Mrs. Gaffney. After getting everything we needed, Bree and I headed back to the ER.

"You shouldn't have any problem with Dr. Ryder," Bree assured me. "He's a nice guy."

"Good," I said. "I just hope he remembers Ted and Lucy coming in that night."

"I'm sure someone will remember. Where's Avis today?"

"He's in court all day." I pulled the list Tanya gave me from my file folder and read down through the names. "You know any of these people?"

"Most of them. Three of them aren't here anymore."

"Are any of them working today?"

"I saw Dr. Ryder earlier." Bree craned her neck to see the other names. "Joyce Jones is here today, and so is Laura Huntly."

"Who do you think has the best memory?"

"Let's talk to Joyce first."

"So what did you think of Mark's meatloaf last night? Pretty good, right?"

"It was really good, Jake."

"He's a good kid, isn't he?"

"Yes. He seems like a good kid."

"I told you so."

We rounded the corner into the ER. "Joyce, you got a second?" Bree called out.

A tall thin black woman, standing next to a bed, was just releasing a blood pressure cuff from a young boy's arm. She removed the stethoscope from her ears and draped it over her shoulders. "Yeah, Bree," she said, putting up a finger. "One second." Bree turned to another woman who was standing at the nurses station. "Mya, have you seen Dr. Ryder?"

The young woman looked around the immediate area. "He was just here," she said.

"What's up, Bree?" Joyce Jones asked.

Bree turned to Joyce. "Joyce, this is my husband Jake, he's a detective with the police department."

Joyce held out her hand and smiled. "It's a pleasure to meet you," she said.

"It's nice to meet you, too" I returned.

"Would it be okay if he asked you a few questions?" Bree asked.

"Sure," Joyce replied.

I opened my file folder, pulled out photographs of Ted and Lucy Gaffney, and laid them on the nurses station, side by side. Do you recognize either of these two?" I asked.

Joyce leaned in for a closer look. "The gentleman looks very familiar."

"The gentleman is Ted Gaffney. He and his daughter—the girl in the other photograph—brought in *his* wife a little over a year ago. She had had a heart attack at home. Instead of calling an ambulance, Mr. Gaffney decided to bring her to the hospital himself, thinking it would save time."

Joyce began slowly nodding her head. "That's right. She didn't make it. I remember. The young girl was yelling at her father for not calling an ambulance. They had car trouble, or something."

"No," came a voice from behind me. "It wasn't car trouble. Someone ran them off the road."

Bree and I turned. "Are you sure, Laura?" Bree asked.

"I'm positive," Laura answered.

"Jake, this is Laura Huntly," said Bree. "She was also on duty that night."

"He said someone ran them off the road?" I asked.

"Yes," Laura replied. "He said he tried to pass a slow moving vehicle, but the person kept swerving back and forth from lane to lane, and wouldn't let them by. When he finally came up alongside the other car, the guy swerved and ran them off the road."

I pointed at the photographs. "And you're positive this is that man?"

"I'm sure of it."

"He didn't mention what type of car it was, did he?" I asked.

Laura shook her head. "If he did, I don't remember."

"Thanks for your help," I said.

Laura turned and went back to work; so did Joyce Jones. I turned to Bree. "What time does the allergy center close?"

"Ten," Bree replied.

"Gaffney brought his wife in at nine-forty-five," I said. "Let's head back over to HR and see if Wanda Truman was working that night."

"You're thinking the driver of that car was John Truman."

"I am."

Chapter Thirty-Four

It was four thirty that same afternoon when Lint and I showed up at Ted Gaffney's front door. I knocked, and a few seconds later Lucy Gaffney opened the door; she was dressed in her cheer leading uniform. She was smiling when she pulled the door open, but that smile quickly faded when she saw it was us.

"What do you want?" Lucy asked, snidely.

"Is your father at home?" I asked.

"Why do you want him?"

"Is he here?" Lint asked.

Lucy rolled her eyes. "Just a second." She left the door standing wide open when she walked away.

A few moments later Ted came to the door. He also asked what we wanted, but not in as bitchy of a tone.

"Can we come in, Mr. Gaffney?" I asked.

"Sure," he replied, and stepped back from the door. He motioned toward the sofa and said, "Have a seat."

We walked inside and Lint shut the door behind us. Neither one of us walked toward the sofa.

"We spoke with two nurses who were on duty when you brought your wife into the emergency room," I stated. "They told us you were run off the road by another car on your way to the hospital that night."

"Why were you asking them about me?" Ted asked.

"Were you run off the road?" Lint asked.

Ted looked back over his shoulder at his daughter. "Lucy, go in the other room," he said.

Lucy stepped back a few steps. "What's the matter, Dad?" she asked.

"We checked Department of Transportation highway footage, Mr. Gaffney. It was John Truman who ran you off the road."

"But you already knew that," Lint added, "because you work at the Department of Motor Vehicles and you looked up his license plate number."

"How do you know that?" Ted asked.

"We don't know *for sure*," I said. "But we'll be able to get a warrant, and whether you looked it up at home or at work we'll know for sure soon enough."

Ted's mouth hung open, but he said nothing.

"You killed Wanda Truman to get even with her husband," I surmised. "You blamed him for your wife's death."

"I looked it up, but—"

"Turn around and put your hands behind your back," Lint said, as he reached for his handcuffs.

"I didn't do anything."

"No!" Lucy screamed, and ran from the room.

Lint placed the cuffs on Gaffney. "You have the right to remain silent. Anything you say can be used against—" Lint paused as he stared over Gaffney's shoulder.

Lucy stood in the middle of the living room, crying. In her hand was a lead pipe, about two feet long. The elbow at one end bore a telltale bloodstain. "I did it," she confessed.

"Lucy," Ted gasped. "No."

"I'm sorry, but I couldn't just let him get away with what he did to us," said Lucy. Tears rolled down her cheeks. For the first time she seemed like a real kid, with real feelings, instead of a spoiled brat. I almost felt sorry for her. Almost.

"Drop the pipe on the floor, Lucy" I said softly.

Lucy complied, and I cuffed her hands behind her back.

Chapter Thirty-Five

I sat in my recliner doing the crossword puzzle. Mark had walked down the street earlier in the day and purchased the paper, and then left it folded to the puzzle on the end table. Bree sat at one end of the couch with her feet pulled up under her, and a magazine opened and balanced on her knee. Mark sat at the other end watching the television. The sliding glass door was open and a nice breeze brought the smell of salt air into the living room.

The TV was tuned to Grit. The manly man retro network. Chuck Norris, the manly manliest man of all, was kicking ass on *Walker, Texas Ranger*.

"So, it was the cheerleader," Bree commented. "I bet that made you happy."

Mark gave her a strange look.

"It figures," I replied. "Most cheerleaders are evil. The ones who don't slay vampires, I mean."

Bree laughed.

Mark stared at the two of us with a confused look on his face.

"Jake hates cheerleaders," Bree informed him.

"Oh," Mark replied. "Why is that?"

"Don't want to talk about it," I said.

"He was in tenth grade," said Bree.

"Enough," I said.

Bree cupped her hand around her mouth and directed her voice in Mark's direction. "Let's just say Jake got caught with his pants down and several other students were pointing and laughing."

"*Tricked* into pulling my pants down," I corrected.

"Jake says cheerleaders are really sirens in disguise and can talk men into doing anything," Bree said.

Mark laughed. "He could be onto something there."

"Terry Blasting is dead because of her," I said. "It was Lucy who gave Terry the pistol, not Wanda Truman. Terry lied to protect Lucy. Lucy tried to get Terry to kill Wanda for her. When he couldn't do it, she took matters into her own hands. Then when Terry ended up getting killed, Lucy tried to make it look like it was all him. Terry really was at the Gaffneys' house until eleven. When he went home, Lucy went to the Truman's and killed Wanda, hitting her in the head with a pipe she found in the Truman's garage."

"How did Lucy get Wanda in the swimming pool?" Bree asked.

"According to Lucy's confession, Wanda was already in the pool," I said. "Out for a midnight swim, apparently."

"Where did Lucy get the gun she gave to the Blasting kid?" asked Mark.

"She bought it from a kid who sells weed at their school," I replied. "We picked him up earlier this evening."

"Case closed," Bree announced, and shut her magazine. "Well, I'm going to bed."

Mark stretched his arms up over his head. "Yeah, me too."

"I'll be right in," I said. "I'm just going to work on this crossword a little longer."

I watched the credits roll over the top of my newspaper and then dozed off.

It was almost midnight when I woke up and shut off the television. I climbed out of my La-Z-Boy, turned off the lamp, and went to the bedroom. I slipped off my pants and got into bed, being careful not to wake Bree. I lay on my back staring at the ceiling. The blinds were open and the moon was bright. Even with my eyes closed I could see the brightness through my eyelids. I thought about getting up and closing the blinds but I was already comfortable. I finally drifted off to sleep.

I don't know what awakened me two hours later. I don't know if it was a sound, or a movement, or the brightness of the moon, but something made me open my eyes. Patch Bowie was standing next to our bed with a sawed-off double barreled shotgun in his hands.

I rolled toward the nightstand.

"Don't," Patch said, and I heard the hammer click.

I slowly rolled back.

"You set my boy up," Patch said.

"Jake?" Bree said.

"Don't move, Bree," I said as calmly as possible. I thought about the sliding glass door that I forgot to shut when I came to bed. "Don't do this, Bowie."

Bowie put the shotgun to his shoulder and trained it on Bree. "You kin watch your little wifey die first," I heard Patch say. "Then it's your turn."

The gunshot sounded like an explosion.

Time slowed as the front of Bowie's shirt ripped open, sending blood and flesh into the air. He fell dead across our legs.

Mark Goodin stood in the bedroom doorway, my 9mm in his hands. "Is he dead?" Mark asked.

"Probably," I said.

Bree didn't move; she just lay there staring at the ceiling. "Mark," she said.

"Yes, Mrs. Stellar?"

"You stay with us as long as you like."

"Thank you, Mrs. Stellar."

Coming Soon:

On the Wagon
From the Tales of Dan Coast

From Bad to Worse
Sunrise City 2

No Enemies Here
From the Tales of Dan Coast

ALSO BY RODNEY RIESEL

Sleeping Dogs Lie
From the Tales of Dan Coast

A mystery set in the Florida Keys follows Dan Coast, an unlicensed private detective of sorts, as he is hired to find the missing boyfriend of a woman who herself soon ends up missing. When someone from the woman's past unexpectedly shows up at Dan's home, with a story of faked deaths and missing life insurance money; Dan along with his sidekick Red set out to find the money, and the woman.

ISBN: 978-0-9883503-0-4

Ocean Floors
From the Tales of Dan Coast

The second installment in the Dan Coast series, Ocean Floors, is a tale of mystery and possible romance when a chance meeting with a beautiful young woman leads Dan and his trusted sidekick Red down a road of murder and kidnapping. Join Dan and Red as they try to solve the murder while searching for a missing friend.

ISBN: 978-0-9894877-0-2

North Murder Beach
A Jake Stellar Novel

The first installment of the story of North Myrtle Beach police detective, Jake Stellar. The spring bike rallies have ended, the spring breakers have all gone back to school, and the summer tourist season is a few weeks away. What better time for a police officer to take a nice quiet relaxing week off from work? That's what Jake Stellar had in mind. That is until someone from his past resurfaces to remind him of a terrible secret he has spent years trying to forget. In North Murder Beach, a story of revenge, Jake is unwillingly and violently forced to confront his secret from his past.

ISBN: 978-0-9894877-1-9

The Coast of Christmas Past
From the Tales of Dan Coast

Coast of Christmas Past is the third book in the Dan Coast series of books. Dan Coast is all set to spend Christmas just the same way he has every year for the past few years; alone and drunk. But when uninvited, unexpected guests arrive and throw a wrench into his holiday plans he is forced to sober up (slightly), and throw on a smile. Just when it seems nothing else could go wrong, a close friend is injured in what appears, to the police, to be a drug deal gone bad. Dan Coast and his sidekick, Red jump into action to find the truth while their friend lies unconscious in the hospital.

ISBN: 978-0-9894877-3-3

The Man in Room Number Four
The Dunquin Cove Series

When a mysterious stranger arrives in the small coastal town of Dunquin Cove, Maine it appears as though Claire and her young son, Mica's prayers have been answer.

But who is he, and why is he really here? Join Claire and her guests at the Colsome House Bed and Breakfast as they piece together the mystery of the Man in Room Number Four.

ISBN: 978-0-9894877-2-6

Ship of Fools
From the Tales of Dan Coast

Ship of Fools is the fourth book in The Tales of Dan Coast series and begins where Coasts of Christmas Past left off. Find out how Dan deals with the death of a young friend, while looking into the disappearance of a new friend's sister. Join Dan, Red, and Skip as they fumble their way through a new mystery.

ISBN: 978-0-9894877-4-0

Beach Shoot
A Jake Stellar Series

It's a beautiful Sunday morning in North Myrtle Beach and Emily Bowen, a wife and mother of four, lies dying on the beach. Jake Stellar returns in Beach Shoot, a new mystery by Rodney Riesel.

Beach Shoot is the second Jake Stellar book and sequel to the Amazon Best Seller North Murder Beach. In Beach Shoot, Jake finds himself teamed up with the most unlikely of partners, his nemesis and fellow detective Avis Lint. Join Jake and Avis as they piece together the clues in this thrilling new mystery.

ISBN: 978-0-9894877-5-7

Return to Dunquin Cove
The Dunquin Cove Series

It's been almost six months since the day ex-hitman, Ben Dunning turned up in Dunquin Cove, Maine, not knowing where or who he was. He's lived a quiet, peaceful life in the small town, but now his old life is calling him back. As Ben plans a trip to Boston in search of his past, little does he know that trouble is brewing in Dunquin Cove. Two strangers have arrived with the promise of safety and security. Join Ben and the people of Dunquin Cove as they band together to prove they can take care of themselves and their town.

ISBN: 978-0-9894877-7-1

Double Trouble
From the Tales of Dan Coast

Shortly after Walter and Warren Bowman arrive in Key West in search of a sister they never knew they had, Warren disappears. With nowhere else to turn, Walter enlists the help of Dan Coast. Join Dan as he and sidekick Red Baxter search for the missing Bowman family members, while dealing with the fallout of an ongoing case.

ISBN: 978-0-9894877-9-5

When Death Returns
A Jake Stellar Series

Has a serial killer from the past returned to North Myrtle Beach? Jake Stellar is back in When Death Returns. Join Jake and his partner Avis Lint in this exciting third installment of the Jake Stellar series as they investigate a homicide that eerily echoes the past.

ISBN: 978-0-9971149-0-4

From Here to There: A Collection of Short Stories

Within this book is a collection of short stories I have written over the past few years. The stories were mostly inspired by trips I've taken, places I've stayed, and conversations I've overheard from Maine to Florida. Although these stories differ from ones I have released in the past, I hope you will enjoy reading them as much as I enjoyed writing them.

ISBN: 978-0-9971149-1-1

Most Likely to Die

From the Tales of Dan Coast

How does someone with no enemies end up murdered? That's for Dan Coast and his sidekick Red Baxter to find out. Join Dan and Red, along with Skip Stoner and Dan's childhood hero, former astronaut, Kip Larson as they piece together the clues that may free an innocent man. In this action packed, sixth installment of The Tales of Dan Coast Series, Dan digs into a wrongly accused man's past and finds out he may not be so innocent.

ISBN: 978-0-9971149-2-8

The Obedience of Fools
A Jake Stellar Series

Join Detective Jake Stellar and his partner, Detective Avis Lint in this fast paced, North Myrtle Beach based Jake Stellar Series. In this fourth installment, The Obedience of Fools, Jake and Avis butt heads with some of The Grand Strand's elite as they try to uncover a secret that may hold the answer to a string of recent homicides.

ISBN: 978-0-9971149-3-5

Deadly Moves
From the Tales of Dan Coast

Dan Coast has finally bought himself a new car, well, new to him. But when he returns to pick up his new ride, he gets an unwanted surprise. In Deadly Moves, the seventh installment in the Tales of Dan Coast Series, we also see the return of Officer Mel Gormin. Join Dan, Red, Mel, and Skip as they do their best to solve the murder of an elderly couple while working as bodyguards to a young starlet who is visiting Key West.

ISBN: 978-0-9971149-4-2

Sunrise City

Cole Ballinger is a retired Fort Pierce police detective and the owner of the Breakwater Bar and Grill. Cole has spent the last ten years doing his best to avoid contact with his ex-wife, but that's easier said than done when she lives in the same town and they have 3 children together. Now Cole's ex has asked for a favor: look into the violent murder of an old acquaintance.

ISBN: 978-0-9971149-6-6

www.ingramcontent.com/pod-product-compliance
Lightning Source LLC
Chambersburg PA
CBHW071855220626

47052CB00002B/133